The Shadow Order

Michael Robertson

Newsletter:
www.michaelrobertson.co.uk

Email: subscribers@michaelrobertson.co.uk

Edited by:
Aaron Sikes - http://www.ajsikes.com
Terri King - http://terri-king.wix.com/editing
And
Pauline Nolet - http://www.paulinenolet.com

Cover Design by Dusty Crosley

Formatting by Polgarus Studio

The Shadow Order is a work of fiction. The characters, incidents, situations, and all dialogue are entirely a product of the author's imagination, or are used fictitiously and are not in any way representative of real people, places or things.

Any resemblance to persons living or dead is entirely coincidental.

Chapter One

A white flash of light exploded across Seb's vision. The Mandulu hit him so hard it felt like the entire planet shifted beneath his feet. With the copper taste of his own blood in his mouth, Seb shook his head and blinked several times before he could focus on the large creature. At a good couple of feet taller than Seb, the average Mandulu towered over him. As wide as they were tall, they had arms and legs like tree trunks and skin like leather. The one in front of Seb—pumped up and breathing heavily—had a larger frame than average for his species. Broken off stumps that used to be horns protruded from his bottom jaw up over his top lip, and scars criss-crossed all over his face; he looked like he'd been in a fight with a glass factory.

With his hand against his cheek like it could offer some comfort, Seb opened and closed his throbbing jaw. "What was *that* for?"

The big dumb creature rolled his shoulders as he rocked from side to side. When he spoke, his voice came out like thunder and vibrated through Seb's chest. "They say you're tough, human." To watch the creature's lips move completely out of sync with the sounds that Seb heard always threw him off. Seb dropped his attention to the floor and listened to how the language chip—a standard that every being that travelled had implanted beneath its skin—manipulated the creature's voice so it came to Seb in words he understood.

A quick glance around the dirty and dark bar, and Seb saw the collection of faces that stared back at him. He was at a spaceport, so he saw many species he didn't recognise, but from the way they looked back, it seemed that most of them recognised him. A notorious reputation for having such a short fuse would do that. He shrugged, his voice loud in what had become the near silence of the bar. "*They?*"

The Mandulu didn't respond. Instead, he deepened his frown and grunted.

"Come on, Seb," Mia Lagos said as she pulled on his arm.

Seb looked at her. The last time he'd seen Mia they were fifteen and at school together. In the near decade since that time, the girl had transformed into a swan, and she smelled better than anything Seb had encountered in a long time. No way could he let the dumb creature disrupt the chance encounter with this floral-scented beauty. A sharp nod and he turned his back on the Mandulu. "You're right; this piece of crap doesn't need my attention." After he'd lifted his glass from the brushed metal bar, he nodded at the pretty girl. "To high school reunions."

Just as Seb went to take a sip of his drink, the Mandulu pulled on his left shoulder and spun him around. The metal tankard flew from Seb's hand and landed in the sawdust on the floor. The beast stared at Seb, huffing and puffing in his fury and waiting for Seb to accept the fight with raised fists. Instead,

Seb yawned and looked around him. Although this place was the best bar in the spaceport, it remained a bar in the spaceport nonetheless. No matter where you went, the mixture of alcohol and many different species had to end in violence. Bala, the bar owner, had constructed the entire place from metal and had bolted every piece of furniture to the floor. Although the only things able to get damaged in a bar brawl were the bodies of the ones brawling, Bala still hated the violence; he cited it as bad for business. Not that you could go anywhere in any spaceport without aggro.

Instead of looking at the Mandulu, who clearly wanted nothing more than to be noticed by him, Seb watched his drink soak into the sawdust floor and shook his head. "Look, pal, just buy me a new drink and move on, yeah?"

The Mandulu's chest rattled with his respiration as if he had a loose flap in his large lungs. He fixed on Seb with his red eyes, his shoulders lifting and falling with each inhale and exhale.

Mia pulled on Seb's arm again, but he didn't look at her this time. "Come *on*," she said, "let's move away."

"I'm not going anywhere," Seb said, more to the Mandulu than Mia. "The punch I can forgive; Mandulus are stupid and act without thought. But my drink ..."

The Mandulu's red eyes shifted from Seb to Mia and back to Seb again. "Maybe you should listen to the little tart and move on. A pretty thing like that gives you a good reason to walk away. Who wouldn't go with her rather than have a fight?" He focused on Mia for a second. "I'll tell you what, sweetheart, if you want to wait until this is all wrapped up, *I'll* go with you."

"Look, Seb," Mia said, blushing and with a warble in her

voice, "this piece of garbage really doesn't matter. Walk away."

The girl made sense, but at nearly twenty-five, Seb had never backed down from a fight … ever. Nevertheless, he thought maybe he should; he gained nothing from fighting other than more grief.

"Your reputation spans the galaxy," the Mandulu said. "The toughest warrior there is. It's the sole reason I came here." Contempt hung from the monster's features as he looked Seb up and down. "I shouldn't listen to rumour, should I? You're clearly a good storyteller, but nothing more."

The temperature of Seb's body rose by a few degrees and his heart rate increased. A glance around the bar and he now saw faces he recognised. Each one of them looked back at him with the same resigned expression. They'd seen it all before. He'd have to teach the Mandulu piece of crap a lesson before he got the message. When Seb looked at Mia, she wore the same imploring expression. Seb hooked a thumb toward the Mandulu. "But look at this thing. He seems like he needs his sense of self-importance beaten out of him. Although from the look of his tusks—"

"Horns," the Mandulu interrupted.

"When you look at his *tusks*," Seb said, "you can see he's already had the snot beaten out of him several times at least." A pause as he drank in the silence around him and Seb snorted a laugh. "Although, I'd say a lot more. Did you know these brutes see it as a sign of strength to have their little tusks broken? I'd be more fearful of the ones with their tusks still intact. Surely that means they don't get hit as much. A pretty fighter is much deadlier than an ugly one." When Seb looked at his reflection in the shined piece of metal behind the bar, half of his face already swollen from the whack he'd received, he brushed his hair over to one side and cocked an eyebrow.

"Walk away," Mia said again.

Seb only knew of the Mandulu's next punch when it rocked his world again. The bar tilted to one side and his legs weakened. Maintaining a reputation shouldn't matter, but the thing had hit him twice now. He couldn't let him get away with it.

The Mandulu lifted his large arms above his head and spun on the spot. "The great Seb Zodo. Feared throughout the galaxy, and when *I* come to fight him, the truth of it is revealed. He's nothing but a pathetic little human. A mama's boy."

Every muscle in Seb's body tensed, and he balled his hands into fists. With the sound of his own pulse as a wet throb in his ears, he drew heavy breaths through his nose. After he'd stared at the ugly Mandulu for a few more seconds, he glanced over at Bala, just about able to focus through his rage.

The bar's owner had his hand over a blaster on the bar as he stared back at Seb. He then nodded in the direction of the door and growled, "Take it outside."

After a long exhale, which did little to prevent the shake that ran through him, Seb pointed at the bar's exit. "Nobody talks about my mum. You want this? We go outside."

Chapter Two

The large open space in front of the bar had seen so many fights—a lot of them involving Seb—that the dark rock surface bore the signs of repeated bloodstains.

When Bala turned the floodlights on, they lit up the ring of smugglers, cargo workers, and pilots that had formed around Seb and the Mandulu. Seb recognised many of the faces as bar regulars and saw several beings flitting in and out of the crowd, taking bets. The touts would give him a percentage of their earnings when he won. He always won.

As he ground his swollen jaw, Seb watched the Mandulu. The large creature swayed from side to side and lowered its brow in Seb's direction. It might have been powerful and have skin like armour, but it didn't have Seb's talent.

"I only came out for a drink tonight," Seb said with a raised voice.

The Mandulu continued to stare and didn't reply.

Now he had the crowd's attention, Seb milked it. "Why can't I enjoy my leisure time without some alpha male trying to challenge me because of rumours they've heard?" When Seb looked to the side and saw a group of Mandulus handing large bags of coins over to one of the touts, he smiled. He'd earn well tonight.

The atmosphere thickened with anticipation, and the Mandulu opposite Seb visibly grew more agitated. The dumb creature bounced on its toes and swayed like a tree in a hurricane, its heavy fists and thick arms swinging down in front of it.

After another glance at the crowd, Seb saw the touts had stopped taking bets. When he looked back at the Mandulu, he drew a deep breath and nodded. Everything around him disappeared. At that moment, nothing else existed other than him and the Mandulu. Seb widened his stance, bent his knees, and beckoned the large creature toward him.

The second the creature moved, Seb's world flipped into slow motion. The Mandulu's heavy steps shook the ground Seb stood on as if a deep bass note ran through it, and the creature's roar resonated as a long drawn-out wall of noise.

As Seb stared into the dark pit of the creature's mouth, its two stumpy horns like jagged rocks wedged in its gums, he caught a whiff of the creature's breath. The rich tang of rotting food smothered him and tied his guts in knots.

Just before the Mandulu reached him, Seb's focus went to its chin. Everything remained in slow motion, so when the beast took a step closer, Seb stepped to the side and drove his fist across the monster's jaw.

The second he made contact with the Mandulu's leathery skin, the crack of his punch coincided with his world speeding up again. The roar of the crowd damn near deafened Seb as he returned to everyone else's pace and watched the Mandulu take three wobbly steps before it hit the ground chin first, its arms limp by its sides.

With his guard still raised, adrenaline surged through Seb and he panted as he watched the unconscious monster lie on the floor. After a couple of seconds, he looked at the crowd, especially the Mandulus who'd bet against him, and raised his arms with a roar. The crowd erupted.

***

When everything settled down, Seb drew a breath as he stepped out in front of the crowd. He opened his mouth, but before he got a single word out, what felt like a million volts surged through his slim form from a point in his lower back. Several violent snaps threw his arms out in front of him in aggressive spasms. A second later, Seb fell flat on his face.

Once on the ground, he rolled over and looked up at the policeman. Tense aggression twisted through the officer's face as he stood over Seb with a taser in his hand. Seb groaned. A second later, the officer dragged Seb to his feet. "Come on," Seb protested, "look at the thing, it's twice my size."

The officer looked at the unconscious Mandulu and then back to Seb. "You're kidding me, right?"

Seb shrugged. "It had to be worth a try."

The officer wrapped cuffs so tightly around Seb's wrists they bit into his skin. "You're coming with me. I've had enough of your crap."

Chapter Three

The car might have hovered a few inches above the ground, but the cushion of air between vehicle and road did little to make the journey comfortable. With the amount of potholes and craters along the dusty track, even the most modern of vehicles had a bumpy journey. The police force didn't use the most modern of vehicles—cheap bastards; all of their cars smelled of sweet snacks and stale sweat.

Drained at the prospect of what he had to face, Seb sat in the passenger seat and bounced around as he looked out the window at the dark and dusty plains of Danu.

"When are you going to stop fighting, boy?"

Only a handful of people could get away with calling Seb 'boy'. Officer Logan—a Frant from a planet Seb could never pronounce—resided in that handful. An older police officer, he'd served on the force with Seb's dad. Unlike the jumped-up prick that arrested him, Logan wanted to do right by people rather than add another notch to his baton.

After a few moments of silence, Seb finally looked across and replied, "I dunno."

"You sound like a moody teenager. How old are you now?"

For a second, Seb stared at the side of the officer's face and clenched his fists. He soon released them, dropped his head, and spoke to his lap. "Twenty-four."

When Seb felt a large hand on his shoulder, he looked up again. In a car that had been designed for the average human, Logan sat folded up in it like a pipe cleaner wedged into a matchbox. The average Frant stood at around seven feet tall. Logan stood even taller than that. Long-limbed, the Frants had slightly pinker skin than humans and breathed through gills in their necks. Soft eyes stared at Seb. "I'm asking these questions because I care."

The tension of moments before melted away in the face of this Frant's kindness. If only his dad had the compassion of Logan. Seb sighed. "I know you do."

***

When they stopped outside Seb's dad's house, Seb looked across at Logan. Although he lived here, it had always been—and would continue to be—his dad's house.

The older officer shook his head as he looked out at the small building in the middle of the plain. Night had settled in, making the already isolated house appear even more lonesome. "How do you live this far away from the city? Don't you get cabin fever out here on your own?"

As they sat stationary, the wind rocked the car from side to side. Other than the house, there was nothing for miles around to block the elements. Some days the wind would blow so strong it would knock Seb to the ground. Every few hours they would have to close the shutters on the windows against an oncoming sandstorm—if they had even bothered to open them at all that day. Most of the time they kept them closed to save the hassle. It shut out both the storms and the daylight.

"Dunno," Seb finally said. "I wouldn't choose it, but I don't have the money to make choices at the moment. I suppose you learn to enjoy the solitude and get used to grit in your eyes."

Logan's eyebrows rose and pinched in the middle. The old Frant might never have said anything, but Seb could tell that he knew how he'd suffered since his mum had died. There were very few people in this life that Seb's dad let into his inner circle—hell, Seb existed outside of it most of the time—but Officer Logan had a free pass whenever he wanted it. Because of their time together on the force, Logan and Seb's dad were tight, so tight that Logan probably knew more about Seb's family than Seb did.

When Logan popped the car's door open with a *click*, the wind rushed in and swirled through the small space. It tousled Seb's hair and threw grit in his eyes. Trained in avoiding the blinding that happened outside on the plains of Danu, Seb squinted, which kept out the worst of it. Before he opened his door, he pulled his goggles from his pocket and put them on.

It would have been easier to walk in the front door, go to his room, and forget about another miserable night where he'd gotten arrested, but Logan insisted on knocking.

As they stood on the porch, grit sprayed the reinforced glass windows on the house, and Seb heard his dad's heavy footsteps walk up the hallway to the door. Seb's shoulders lifted to his neck and a rock clamped in his stomach in anticipation of what would come. Despite being twenty-four, his dad reduced him to a teenager every time he voiced his displeasure at him.

The door yanked open in front of them, revealing the usual frown of disappointment that Seb associated with his dad. After he held Seb's stare for a few more seconds, he turned to Logan and spoke with a sigh. "Hi, Logan, how are you?"

Logan and Seb's dad shook hands. The Frant's larger palm enveloped even Seb's father's big grip. "I'm sorry to do this, Joe."

As he shot a scowl at Seb, his dad shook his head. "Not as sorry as I am. It seems like my boy's a drain on the station's resources."

"My main concern," Logan said, "is that I won't be able to keep bailing him out. McGovern wanted to hang him out to dry for this one, but I called in a favour. I don't have many left."

It started with the slight widening and then relaxing of his jaw as Seb's dad tensed up. Within a few seconds, he moved his mouth as if he chewed something other than the bitter taste of disappointment. The man always did it when he got angry. It usually stopped him from shouting in front of people, but he looked at Seb like he wanted to kill him. After a lingering glare, he turned back to Logan, and his features softened slightly. "I don't want you to call in any more favours for him. You've given him a chance, and he has to learn his lesson. I'm guessing he was fighting again?"

Instead of a reply, Logan dipped his head and looked down at the ground.

Seb's dad sighed again. "The boy needs to learn. If that means prison ..."

"I *am* here, you know," Seb said as he stepped forward.

Both Seb's dad and Logan looked at him, and then his dad spoke. "We can see that, Seb. That doesn't mean we won't talk about you. You're nearly twenty-five and you still behave like a child. You've caused me enough headaches in your life, and I can't keep on taking responsibility for you. I don't need it any more. Especially not now."

"Why's now any different?"

Silence hung between the three men, and Seb's dad looked out into the darkness of the plains. A glisten of tears coated his dark eyes and he drew another deep breath. A man of few words, he had enough sighs in him to out-puff the winds of Danu.

"Look, Seb," Logan said, "we know you collect a purse for every fight. We know the bookies throw a percentage your way. Everyone knows that. If you get nicked again, the police will use that against you. I shouldn't tell you this, but they have the evidence now. If you get tried for illegal gambling, you won't see the light of day for a long time."

At first, Seb wanted to deny the money, but when he looked at his two elders, he saw the futility in it. "Sure," he finally said, "I'm broke and the money helps, but I didn't fight him for the money."

"They won't believe that," Logan said.

When he looked back at his father's disappointed face, Seb forced his words past the lump in his throat. "The guy mentioned Mum."

A shake of his head and Seb's dad looked even more disappointed. Another one of his signature sighs and he stared at the ground. When he looked back up, his eyes were bloodshot, almost as if he'd been crying—not that his dad ever cried. Even when Seb's mum had died, he just went quiet … permanently. "You can't flip out every time someone mentions Mum. She's dead, Seb; deal with it like we've all had to."

The words stung and Seb didn't reply.

"Besides," his dad said, "how do you think it would make Mum feel to know you're fighting because some idiot mentioned her to you in a pub? You can't hide behind that excuse anymore. You fight because you can't manage your ego. You want to prove to the world that you're a big man. If you learned to walk away, you wouldn't get into any of this trouble and people would respect you more. You're a damn clown, Seb, and despite what you think you look like, a clown is all the world sees of you."

It didn't matter how many times he tried to reason with his dad, the man wouldn't listen. He had an opinion on everything and nothing could change it. Instead, Seb turned sideways and moved past his dad to get into the house. His feet echoed against the wooden floor in the hallway as he walked up it.

"Aren't you going to apologise to Logan?" Seb's dad said.

"Why? He's brought me here. To you! I'd get a warmer welcome in police custody. All I get here are looks of disappointment and reminders that my mum is gone. Here, I have to face the bitter reality that the wrong parent got taken from me far too soon."

Guilt dragged on Seb's frame because of the last comment, but he continued to walk away. Life *would* have been better if his dad had died instead of his mum.

Although his dad spoke again, he didn't talk to Seb. Instead, he exchanged pleasantries with Logan that Seb couldn't make out even if he'd wanted to.

The front door slammed by the time Seb reached the kitchen, and he jumped clean off the ground at the loudness of it. He couldn't see his dad from where he stood, but he heard his heavy steps come up the hallway toward him.

Chapter Four

By the time his dad reached the kitchen, Seb had picked up a mowgrove fruit and taken a large bite. So ripe it nearly exploded when he sank his teeth into it, Seb let the juice run down his chin and onto the floor. His dad could deal with the mess. Besides, it would give him something to moan about, which seemed to be his favourite pastime.

A large man with a strong jaw and a heavy frown, Seb's dad strode up to him in the gloomy kitchen. The pair looked at one another as the wind howled against the closed shutters. The breeze, although outside, still found a way through the cracks and crevices in the wooden structure. It seemed that no matter how well his dad insulated against the elements, the wind always found a way through. Dust and sand got everywhere, and although Seb had gotten used to the feel of it against his skin, it didn't make wearing a layer of grit a pleasant experience.

As Seb took another bite of the mowgrove, his dad threw his arms up in the air and leaned forward, his face red. "When will you stop fighting?"

Now Logan had gone, the true anger of the large man would

be set loose. Although Seb looked at him, he didn't reply.

"Mum wouldn't want this, you know?"

"What do you know about Mum?" With his heart pounding, Seb stepped closer to his dad and stared up at him. "When Mum was alive, all you did was work. You don't know anything about the woman."

"This again? Seriously?"

"What do you expect, Dad? You throw her name around when it suits you, but you weren't there for her. Yeah, you eased your conscience by claiming you had to spend so much time away from the house to support a family, but that wasn't the real reason. You couldn't cope with a family, so you hid at work."

When Seb's dad lifted his large chest, he seemed to rise by a few inches. "That *isn't* true."

"You're emotionally devoid, Dad." As Seb looked around their gloomy kitchen, the *womp, womp, womp* of their generator sounded outside. They lived so far away, they couldn't access the grid. Seb laughed. "Look at where you've chosen to live! In the middle of these plains away from everything and everyone."

His dad's large eyes narrowed. "Not far enough away from you, though."

Sure, the words stung and Seb winced from the attack, but he'd been the focus of his dad's contempt for so long that he'd grown used to the man's bitterness. Besides, he'd told him he should have died instead of his mum, and although it might have worked out better if Seb took it back, he couldn't do it.

"Anyway," Seb said, "why should I stop fighting? I'm good at it." Even at that moment, with his dad almost squaring up to him, Seb could feel the world around him slow down, and he saw the exact spot on his dad's large chin that would drop him like a sack of rocks.

"The only thing you get from it is trouble."

"And money, Dad. Don't forget the money."

"Not enough to move out, though, is it? Or even to give me rent."

As much as he wanted one, Seb didn't have a reply. Having been skint since he'd left school, the money he got from the touts after his fights kept him going until the next fight, and nothing more.

Seb's dad stepped back, sat down on one of the kitchen stools, and dropped his head. "I may not show it, but I do care."

"You're right, Dad, you *don't* show it."

"I worry that what happened to your brother will end up happening to you. I know you're good at fighting, but so was your brother—and he killed a Frant in a fight."

A shake of his head and Seb screwed his face up when he said, "You don't need to keep reminding me. I'm more than aware of what Davey did."

"Do you forget that he's in prison for life? For life! We'll never see him again. That doesn't bother you?"

"Of course it bothers me. I miss Davey something rotten, but I'm *not* him." Seb took another bite of the mowgrove and ran his forearm across his chin to remove the juice that ran down it. "Davey had no control over his anger. When he lost it, nothing could stop him. I'm not like that. I know how to fight." Seb had never told his dad about his talent, and he never would. If anyone would be likely to believe Seb about what happened when he fought, it certainly wouldn't be his old man.

Seb watched his dad's hand shake as he remained perched on the stool and reached over for a glass of water on the work surface. He didn't seem in control of his limbs. Instead of grabbing the glass, he knocked it from the side. As it fell, everything slowed down for Seb. He watched the glass spin on its downward trajectory, and he could have caught it. Instead, he let it hit the dusty wooden floor with a loud *crash.*

With a frown that darkened his view, Seb looked down at the smashed glass and then back up at his dad.

Several heavy breaths and no words as Seb's dad looked back. The same glaze that Seb had seen at the front door ran across his dad's eyes. A withdrawn grief, a need to cry. But his dad ignored it and said, "Why don't you take on an honest profession? Anything."

Seb laughed. "Like law enforcement? Get myself a swell partner so we can both say how bloody great we are as we cruise around on our cloud of self-esteem?"

"It doesn't matter what it is. Get a job in cargo for all I care; just earn an honest wage."

When the man wobbled on his stool, Seb rushed forward to catch him. Before he could, his dad reached out and grabbed the side to steady himself. The words sat in Seb's mouth, but he couldn't ask 'Are you okay?'—especially when he made eye contact with the man and received a fierce glare of hostility in return. A proud man, he wouldn't answer truthfully even if something were wrong. Instead, Seb shrugged off his dad's strange behaviour. "On most planets, fighting *is* an honest wage."

Clearly riled by the comment, Seb's dad roared at him, "Then maybe you should go to one of those planets."

"Why don't you get off my case? You've done nothing but have a go at me for years now. Since Mum died, you've been a complete arsehole."

After he'd shaken his head several times, Seb's dad looked down again with one of his signature sighs. The man deflated with exasperation. When he finally lifted his head, tears glistened on his cheeks. "I'm dying, Seb."

The words reached into Seb's stomach, gripped his bowels, and tore them clean out. "You're *what*?"

"I'm dying. I don't have long left. I didn't want to tell you during an argument, but all we do is argue, so it's not like I could have chosen another time."

Ever since Seb could remember, his dad had worn a thick necklace that looked like a snake around his neck. A gift from Seb's grandfather to his dad before he passed. Whenever his dad felt uncomfortable, he'd absentmindedly fiddle with it. On the day of his mum's funeral, Seb watched him hold it for the entire service. At that moment in the quiet kitchen, he gripped onto the heavy chain like his life depended on it.

Despite the gravity of the situation, Seb didn't see it coming, and when his dad spoke again, Seb lost the strength in his legs.

"The doctor said I'll be dead within a month."

Seb stumbled backwards. Just before he fell to the ground, he grabbed onto the side of the table for stability, pulled a stool toward him, and lowered himself onto it. With the air leaving his body in a withering sigh, Seb stared at his dad and said nothing.

Chapter Five

Two Years Later ...

The muscles in Seb's back burned like they would tear at any moment. Their heaviest cargo yet, Seb shoved the large box the last metre it needed to go before he stood up straight and gasped for breath. The large metal container stood nearly as tall as him. As he stared at it, the layer of sweat that coated his body turned frigid in the cold environment. Sometimes the cargo they carried presented no problems. At other times, like this, it felt like he had to move mountains.

The Bandolin had been a freighter ship for decades and it showed. Even now, after all this time on the ship, Seb looked around the cargo hold and shook his head at the state of the place. Shabby around the edges, the freighter moved slowly and steadily through the galaxy. One of a fleet owned by wealthy transport merchants, it moved whatever needed to be transported from planet to planet. As long as they didn't have to break the law to shift the cargo, anything went, regardless of the strain it put on the workers.

Over a year and half into the job and Seb had hated every minute of it. Today felt no different as he stared at the large box that he hadn't yet moved far enough. He felt ready to admit defeat. Not that they'd let him; if he couldn't do the job, then why did he sign up?

The stale reek of his own effort took Seb back to his first six months of working on *The Bandolin*. In that time, Seb had spent all of his paltry earnings on booze, which he sweated out as he worked through his daily hangovers. Having stood by his father's side as the man died, he'd tried to drink the pain away. It only served to land him in trouble with his employers and make him more dependent on his terrible wage because he had no other finances to get him off the ship. He shouldn't have cared about the old man; after all, he'd even told him that he'd rather he'd died than his mum. But as it turned out, he wasn't as detached from the old bastard as he thought he was.

As punctual as ever, his dad had died within the month he'd been given. Seb didn't leave his house on Danu for the next sixteen weeks. Maybe he would still be there now were it not for Logan. The Frant turned up one day and told Seb he'd signed him up to work on *The Bandolin*. As a way to make some kind of amends with his dead father, Seb took the job.

The silver snake that had once been his dad's hung around Seb's neck, and he stroked it as he rested in the cold space. A shiver snapped through him as he watched several other beings move boxes around in the red glow. As big as his old school's sports hall, the warehouse aboard *The Bandolin* had racks and racks of goods. It took an army of men to run the place around the clock. Their current cargo contained the eggs from a rare creature on a now destroyed planet. Seb had peeked inside and looked at the white leathery shells that stood just a few inches shorter than the huge crates that housed them. When the things hatched, they'd bring chaos with them. The creatures had wings and breathed fire. Apparently, the babies came out all guns blazing. To prevent that from happening, the cargo hold had to be colder than usual; too warm and *The Bandolin* wouldn't make it to its next destination.

Just as Seb thought about continuing with his work, the voice of his boss called through the dark cargo hold. "Oi, you!"

Seb didn't need to look around to know the horrible git meant him. Ever since Seb had been employed to work on *The Bandolin*, his boss, Snart, had treated him like dirt.

At over eight feet tall, the Granth, Snart, weaved through the large boxes, his breath visible as condensation even in the dark red glow of their surroundings. Although the red light made it difficult for Seb, it had been proven to be the most pleasing light for the majority of the species who worked on the ship. Obliged to offer night-vision goggles to all of their workers, Seb had been given a pair that stank of sweat. They still had the slime of their previous wearer on them, and they were so old, they didn't work properly.

"What are you doing?" Snart asked; his voice was so shrill, Seb flinched every time he spoke.

"What do you mean?"

When Snart put his four hands on his hips and stared at Seb, Seb found it hard not to laugh. Regardless of the fact that one of his large hands rested on the handle of his blaster, Seb still found the sight amusing. Little did the dumb creature know that it would only take Seb one well-timed swing and Snart would be out cold. But Seb had left that life behind. Instead, he would put up with Snart's nonsense. With his mirth stuffed down inside of him, Seb waited for Snart to speak again.

"What are you doing?" Snart asked. "It's a question that doesn't need explaining. What. Are. You. Doing?"

Seb hooked a thumb in the direction of the large metal box he'd just moved and said, "Moving boxes."

"Don't get smart with me."

"I'm sorry?"

"You're not moving boxes. You might be *pretending* to move boxes, but it looks to me like you're resting up while everyone else moves boxes."

The shrill words of his boss carried through the cavernous space, and for a moment, every pair of eyes in the room stopped and focused on Seb. "I've just moved a box, Snart. I wanted to take a minute to rest before I move the next one."

"Do you see anyone else resting?"

A glance around the room, and if anyone had been resting before that moment, they certainly weren't now.

Before Seb could reply, Snart said, "You humans aren't cut out for this work. If it were up to me, I wouldn't employ a single one of you. You're weak, slow, and so bloody sensitive to the changing environments. I want workers that are flexible to our needs, not the other way round."

Seb laughed. "All of that on the wage you pay? You don't want much, do you?"

Snart stepped so close, Seb had to breathe through his mouth to stop the creature's sweaty scent from choking him. With just inches separating them, he stared at the Granth's waxy skin and the slimy secretion that coated it. A slow heave rolled through his stomach.

"Look," Seb said, holding up the palm of his right hand at Snart, "maybe humans aren't suited for this kind of work, but you *have* to employ me. You know that, and I know that. You need a certain variation of species aboard your ship to get all the tax relief you can, so don't pretend I don't earn this company money by being here. Humans tend to get better jobs than this, so the way I see it, you need me more than I need you. It'll take you a while to find someone like me who's prepared to put up with your nonsense."

Snart's bulbous jaw looked like a deflated football strapped to his chin. It moved up and down, but no words came out as he clearly looked for a response in his hollow mind. After a few seconds, he reached out and cuffed Seb around the back of the head.

Snart had hands as large as dinner plates, and the heavy blow threw stars across Seb's vision. As he shook it off, he looked at his boss and everything slipped into slow motion. The space beneath Snart's right eye begged to be struck, and Seb balled his hands into fists as he stared at him.

But he refrained. He'd promised his dad he would no longer be led by his ego. Snart challenged that more than anyone he'd met since making the promise, but he had to stick to his word.

Snart cuffed Seb again before he stepped away. "Get back to work before I take disciplinary action against you."

As Snart walked off, Seb continued to stroke his dad's old snake necklace. It gave him the presence of mind to hold back more than anything ever had before.

With his jaw locked so tightly it ran streaks of pain up the side of his face, Seb drew deep breaths and stared at the broad back of his boss. Seb would be compliant … for now.

Chapter Six

No matter where Seb directed his attention to on his body, it ached. Stabbing pains ripped across the back of his shoulders from shoving the large boxes. Sharp pains like broken glass sat in his knees from having to bend down and stand up again so many times. Swollen knuckles made it tricky for him to open and close his grip from where the cold of the air-conditioned cargo bay had worked into his joints.

Seb walked into the canteen at the end of his shift with ginger steps and locked in a permanent wince. He drew shallow breaths to try to ease the nausea in his tense stomach. Another day of moving the massive metal boxes with the eggs in them would break him.

The change from the gloomy red light of the cargo bay to the bright white strip lighting of the dining area burned Seb's eyes, and he blinked several times to clear his blurred vision.

Shuffling like the undead, Seb groaned internally as he made his way through the canteen. He did his best to avoid the further pain of bumping into any one of the many beings that flitted about in the busy space. The culmination of the collective sounds from all of the diners in the packed canteen rose up into the high ceiling and mixed into a disorientating white noise that stabbed at Seb's tired brain.

At the centre of the ship, the canteen took up more space than any sector on *The Bandolin*, other than the cargo bay. Everything in the space had been made from steel like most other parts of the ship. The floor, the walls, the ceiling, the benches that had been bolted into the floor—even the serving hatch the canteen workers handed the food through. In fact, it would be easier to list the things in the canteen that hadn't been made from steel.

Seb joined the long queue waiting for food. Although everyone on the ship shared the same queue, each sector had their own separate dining areas. Some chose to mingle, but it had to be done by mutual consent. As a result, the beings who worked in the cargo bays had to stay put in their grimy corner. The lowest of the low, they bore the label of 'trouble'; and with so many fights and fallings-out in public spaces, who could blame the others for making that judgement of them. There had even been a petition to give the cargo workers a separate area to collect their cutlery and food from, but it had been dismissed as discriminatory.

Although the wall on his left side had been made from cold steel, Seb still leaned against it as he waited in line. Every ten seconds or so, the long string of bodies would shift forward a step and stop again.

So tired from his day, Seb fought against his heavy eyes as he looked at the people around him. Withdrawn into a semi-delirious state, his thoughts slowed to a near halt and not much made sense to him at that moment. He snapped from his daze when Snart and his two cronies appeared, pushed him aside, and moved in front of him in the queue.

Snart rocked from side to side in front of Seb and stared at him with a smug grin on his wide face. The two Mandulus that he always had with him, Wenko and Zenko, were brothers. Like the brute Seb fought in the bar a few years back, the pair had the inflated sense of self that went with being a member of their warrior race. They too stared at Seb as they silently tried to provoke him.

Although the delirium of near sleep had left Seb, he didn't react. Instead, he continued to stare at the three of them and stroked his dad's snake necklace. They wouldn't drag him into a fight in such a crowded area.

The fact that Seb didn't respond seemed to irk Snart, who spoke in a loud voice so everyone could hear. "We're pushing in front because we, unlike you, pull our weight in the cargo bay. You're a lazy good-for-nothing that doesn't deserve to eat, let alone eat before us."

Those in the queue around them looked at Seb. The temperature seemed to increase in the canteen, and Seb pulled on his collar to ease the itch of sweat that ran around it. Still, he did not reply.

"I saw him picking his nose for half of his shift today," one of the brothers said. Wenko … Zenko—Seb could never tell. And he really didn't care to. Both of them had the broken horns that came from their bottom jaw up over their top lips. Both of them were built like large lumps of machinery; both of them would go down like a flower with a broken stem if hit in the correct place. Seb shook his head. He couldn't think like that. No matter how much he wanted to hurt them, he'd made a promise to his dad.

***

For the entire time he'd queued, Seb tolerated the looks and wisecracks from the three creatures in front of him. Their collective weight had to be at least ten times that of Seb's, but the more they pushed him, the more obvious their weak spots became. Both brothers had chins of glass like most of their race, and the space beneath Snart's right eye would drop him like a puppet with its strings cut.

After the three of them had taken their food, Seb took his. The canteen offered very little choice, so Seb never bothered to ask what he'd been served. Mostly stew full of some synthetic roots of one kind or another. Pretty bland, it tasted of salt and it always smelled like gravy, but it had been genetically modified to have the perfect balance of vitamins, minerals, and calories. Since Seb had been on the ship, he'd never been ill.

As Seb walked toward the section of the canteen where the cutlery sat, one of the brothers walked toward him, his focus on something behind Seb. Whatever he wanted, it didn't matter, as long as he got out of Seb's face.

However, at the last minute, the brother's arm shot out and he whacked the bottom of Seb's tray. The loud *crack* snapped through the huge open space to be followed by a *crash* as the tray and Seb's food hit the cold metal floor.

With his usual booming voice, Snart walked over to Seb and spoke so most of the canteen could hear it. "See, this useless piece of dung can't even carry a tray of food. Why are we still paying this fool to work in cargo?"

For a moment, Seb remained on his feet and looked around. It seemed that most of the faces in the place had turned his way. As he drowned in the weight of their collective mirth, Seb shook. His pulse throbbed as a wet boom in his ears and he focused his attention on Snart. The space beneath his right eye, big enough for a fist, screamed to be whacked.

Seb clenched his fists as Snart tilted his head to one side. "Go on, little man, do it."

However, Seb withdrew from his rage, and the prominence of Snart's weak spot pulled away from him. With a heavy sigh that sank through his entire body, Seb hunched down and picked up his ruined lunch.

Accompanied by the sound of what sounded like a thousand different sniggers, Seb placed his plate back on his tray and tried to pick up some of the stew, which had mostly soaked through the holes in the floor.

Because Seb focused on the tidy-up, the first he knew of one of the brothers approaching came with excruciating pain through his left fist as the brute stamped on his hand. The heavy foot, as large as Seb's head, slammed down so hard, something snapped, and a screaming pain instantly ran from his knuckles straight up his forearm.

Seb resisted the urge to howl, left his tray on the ground, and jumped to his feet. He might have had a broken left hand, but as he stepped close to the brother, he balled his stronger right hand into a fist. Heat rushed through Seb's face as he clenched his jaw and looked up at the ugly creature that stood at least two feet taller than Seb.

With a smug and derogatory glare, the beast said, "What?" The boom of his voice hit Seb in the sternum like a hard shove, and he stumbled backwards.

Everything slowed down for Seb, so when the brother repeated his question, it came out as a long bass roll. Overwhelmed by his booming pulse, Seb breathed in through his nose and out through his mouth. Wound as a coiled spring, every ache he'd felt when he'd entered the canteen had vanished.

Despite his rage, Seb managed to pull himself from it, and the world around him returned to normal speed again. The spot on the Mandulu's chin faded away, and the voice of Snart came through clearer than ever.

"You're a waste of space, Seb. Why don't you do us all a favour and quit this job?" The words echoed through the vast hall as the only sound.

Seb looked at the thousands of faces that stared at him and didn't respond.

"Why don't you get dropped off at the next spaceport and earn your living sweeping floors or cleaning toadstools from toenails?"

Some of the beings in the canteen laughed at Snart's words, but Seb held onto his fury. He'd made a promise and he'd stick to it.

"Why don't you go running back home, mama's boy?"

Something—other than one of the bones in his hand—snapped in Seb, and everything flicked back into slow motion.

Chapter Seven

With the world around him at a virtual halt, Seb rushed at Snart. When he got close, he lunged at his boss, his fat and smug face still split with a leering grin. Seb let his broken left hand hang down and caught him with a jab beneath the eye with his right. Ripples ran across the fat Granth's face from the point of impact, and before Seb had pulled his hand away, Snart's piggy eyes had rolled back in his head and he'd started to fall.

Shock hung limp on the faces of the two Mandulus, and before they could react, Seb had landed one punch on each of their weak chins. As their leader had done, they fell like their muscles had failed them.

Seb withdrew from his fighting state to see all three of his antagonisers topple at the same time. Their collective collapse ran a heavy shock through the steel floor.

Now Seb had returned to the normal pace of the canteen, the silence of the place overwhelmed him. Every face looked his way, but the mirth that had previously twisted their features was now gone. Instead, jaws hung loose, eyes spread wide, and gills flared.

Before Seb could say a word, the *thwip* of a spider gun went off. A second later, the sticky net bound him in a grip that crushed the air from his body and knocked him down. With his arms clamped to his sides, Seb's head spun as he lay on the floor, smothered by the toxic reek of the glue used on the ropes.

As Seb lay there with his face squished into the cold metal, the vibration of the rush of heavy boots ran through the floor into his cheek. He looked up to see the ship's security force closing in on him, their blasters raised.

Seb opened his mouth to speak, but before he could say a word, the heavy boot of one of the guards stamped across his chin and turned his lights out.

Chapter Eight

The *whoosh* of *The Bandolin*'s boosters ran a shudder through the entire ship. So powerful they could have burned a hole through most planets, at present they were being used to slowly lower the massive freighter.

As Seb stood by the ship's exit with the captain, he looked down at the strange creature. Blue-skinned, the diminutive Barch stared back. At no more than four feet tall, it seemed odd to be subservient to the thing, but Seb had once seen a Barch fight. One of the few creatures he'd battle reluctantly, he'd seen how their wide mouths opened when they were enraged. The small orifice spread to about a foot in diameter and revealed two rows of razor-sharp teeth that could cut diamonds. Sure, Seb would beat one in a fight if he needed to—especially since they'd fixed his broken hand in *The Bandolin*'s medic bay—but he'd certainly exercise more caution about the fight in the first place. The ship's captain also had a blaster that looked like it could turn a planet to dust, and he had it trained on Seb.

After a quick glance at the weapon, Seb looked back into the captain's yellow eyes. "Can I please stay on board for a little longer? Maybe just give me one more chance?"

When the Barch spoke, it showed Seb its strange dialect in how its lips moved. The language chip meant Seb heard every word of it, but he couldn't take his eyes off the unusual shapes and movements the creature pulled with its mouth. "I can't have you on my ship," the captain said. "You're on the bottom rung on *The Bandolin* and you're fighting with people well above your station. I know Snart's a jackass, but one of you has to go, and he's more important to me than you are. Besides, having a human on board rarely works out, regardless of the tax benefits. Unfortunately, I fear you will forever be reviled because of your species' legacy. To colonise so many planets has made you plenty of enemies, whether that's your fault personally or not."

What an idiot Seb had been! He'd lasted so long putting up with Snart's nonsense. If he'd held it together long enough to get to a spaceport he knew, he could have left on his own terms. His dad had been right about him being a waste of space driven by his ego. Once again, fighting had gotten him into trouble.

Although the monitors by the door were grainy, they gave a clear picture of the spaceport below. Surrounded by water, it seemed to exist as an island in its own right. The strong sun hit the sea and created a glare on the screen. Without taking his eyes off the images, Seb said, "Well, at least tell me where we are."

"This is a place called Aloo."

"And what's it like?"

As an apology, the captain winced when he passed a credit card to Seb.

A glance down and Seb read the card had three hundred credits on it. He looked back up at the ship's captain. "What's this?"

"Your severance package with a month's extra pay on top. We feel bad about leaving you here, but fighting is—"

"Bad for business. I know."

When the small Barch stood aside, Seb stared at the teleport hub and his throat dried. After he'd closed his mouth, he gulped. "I have to use that thing?"

"If we land, Seb, it'll take us twelve hours to refuel and take off again. We can't waste that time."

"But forcing me to teleport?"

"You got yourself into this situation."

For the briefest moment, the world around Seb slowed ever so slightly and the captain's nose stood more prominent on his face than any other part of him. If Seb could whack the captain before he opened his mouth, he'd knock the little cretin out. Although, what then? He couldn't fly the ship. Those aboard would overpower him and force him to teleport, and that was the best case. At least now he had a guaranteed safe landing, well, almost guaranteed. With teleporting, nothing could be guaranteed. At least he had a good chance of not dying. A fight with the captain might see Seb victorious, but it would be bound to end with his death when the rest of the ship turned on him.

Letting out a heavy sigh, Seb stepped into the teleport hub. When the curved glass door rolled shut in front of him, it trapped him inside the booth with nothing but his rucksack and the credit card the captain had given him. He and the captain stared at one another, but Seb didn't plead any more. The cold glare of the Barch told him not to bother.

After a sharp salute, the captain pressed one of his long

fingers on the teleport button. A millisecond later, Seb got dragged backwards by his waist, and his stomach shot into his throat. He tasted bile as his world spun out of control.

Chapter Nine

Seb hit the spaceport's solid ground with such force he fell forward onto his knees. A sharp pain ran through his kneecaps and sent streaks of lightning up his thighs. With his face in his hands, he screamed so loud it tore at his throat. Not only did he have to deal with the agony of a hard landing, but he had to ride out the decompression effects of the teleportation. Tears streamed down his cheeks and his brain felt like it would leak from his nose like snot. With his teeth clenched, he rocked back and forth, oblivious to his surroundings.

It happened slowly, far too slowly for Seb's liking, but he pulled away from his pain, and the world around him came into focus. First, he smelled salt in the air, and the dampness of Aloo's atmosphere wrapped around him. When he sat up, the wind tossed his hair and cut to his core. The bright sun reflected off the water that surrounded the spaceport, and Seb squinted against the glare. Ships sat in rows next to one another with very little space between them. A queue of freighters hovered in the sky as they obviously waited to dock in the busy port.

As Seb got to his feet, a sharp pain inside his skull and a rock of nausea in his stomach, he drew what started out as a deep breath. Halfway in, he stopped and his palms turned damp with sweat. If he pulled much more air into his body, he'd vomit where he stood.

Although busy, the spaceport seemed like a lonely place. Almost every living being around Seb walked at a fast march and stared at the ground. Not a place for socialising.

The loud *boom* as *The Bandolin* broke the sound barrier above snapped through Seb and spiked both his splitting headache and nauseous lump in his guts. One of the biggest ships he'd ever seen, Seb watched his ride home turn into a red dot in the sky. He shook his head. "Damn it."

With his belongings in his bag and a paltry amount on a credit card, Seb stumbled off in search of somewhere to stay.

***

After about a ten-minute walk, Seb found a hotel. The damp wind had thrown so much salty water at him in that time that every exposed part of his flesh stung as if red raw. It felt like he'd been sprayed with broken glass. The very beginnings of sores burned at the corners of Seb's eyes and mouth, and the stench of salt blocked his nose. But he deserved it. Of course he did. If he'd listened to his dad's advice and walked away from the fight with Snart ...

Seb shook his head as he walked up to the front of what seemed to be a hotel. Unfamiliar with the native language of Aloo—he'd never even heard of the place until now—he looked at the large orange letters scrawled across the front of the building. Fortunately, the universal sign for hotel sat next to the words. A house with a nightcap on, it told Seb all he needed to know.

The automatic doors closed behind Seb after he'd entered the hotel's foyer, shutting out the deafening wind and rumble of large freighter engines. Now he stood sheltered inside, Seb shook his head like a wet dog would. It did little to remove the moisture from his hair and face, made his headache worse, and threw him off balance. As he thrust his arms out for stability, he looked up and made eye contact with the lady at the front desk.

Who knew what species she belonged to, the woman had two heads and just one large eye on each face. She smiled two different smiles at him as he walked close. Like looking at someone with a lazy eye, Seb didn't know which face to address, so he picked the smile he liked the most. "Um ... hi. Do you have any spare rooms at the moment?"

"We certainly do. How many nights? One? Two?" Both heads spoke, taking one word each. The change in tone threw Seb off, but they delivered their sentences seamlessly.

"Um ..." Seb looked around the well-lit foyer. The place seemed run-down, beaten by nature's onslaught of salt and wind combined, but it seemed clean. He probably wouldn't find anywhere better. "Indefinitely?"

The woman smiled again. "Sure, let's get you in the slightly cheaper accommodation if that's the case. It'll make your money go a little further."

After he watched the woman tap away at a screen, Seb said, "So, what's Aloo like?"

Although there were no other beings in the reception area, silence descended on the room as if there were, and every one of them had held their breath in response to his question.

Several more taps and the receptionist looked back at Seb. "Huh?"

She'd clearly heard him the first time. Seb raised an eyebrow to show he needed a response.

"It's an interesting place. We have no laws here."

"None?"

The receptionist shook her heads. "Not a single one. We're in one of the farthest away spots in the galaxy, so it's considered intergalactic space. As a result, no one regulates us. No taxes, no police, no army … no prisons."

The words tore Seb's stomach out. He'd landed in the armpit of the galaxy. It took him a second to recover. "So what about work? Is that easy to come by?"

With an expression somewhere between pity and condescension, the receptionist placed a hand on her heart. "Oh, honey, there's no work out here. The only way to get a job is to wait for someone already in one to die. You need to get work on a ship to get out of here, but most captains won't employ someone they don't know—especially if they've met them here. And most especially, if you don't mind me saying …?"

Seb nodded.

"If they're human."

"Figures," Seb said.

"Besides," the receptionist said, "the ships often carry cargo they don't want anyone knowing about, so they all have trust issues."

Before Seb could reply, the receptionist held up a room key and beamed two grins at him. "But good luck. Your room's on the third floor."

Although Seb didn't respond, he took the key from the woman, spun around, and headed to his new room. Quite how long he'd be able to afford the rent for … well, it didn't bear thinking about. To enquire about price at that moment would be a cold, hard reality he could do without.

Chapter Ten

Maybe, in time, Seb would get used to the reek of salt in the air. Surrounded by a vast ocean on the island spaceport, he'd better. Until he got off the cursed planet, he had no other choice.

As he stood in the hotel room he'd been given, Seb took in his surroundings. His assessment of the place based on the foyer had proven to be accurate so far. The room, shabby but clean, had stain-free bed sheets—always a good sign. However, none of the room had been sectioned off, so a toilet sat in one corner alongside a shower. Not a place to bring people back to; Seb hardly wanted to watch someone else use the lavatory.

Several salt-stained glasses sat on the kitchen draining board, so Seb picked one up, filled it with the cloudy water that came from the tap, and held it up to the light. A sign on the wall showed a picture of a running tap with a tick next to it. The fact that they had to assure the guests that the water could be drunk made Seb's stomach tense in anticipation. After a deep breath, he took a sip. The salty burn that he'd anticipated didn't come, but the water had a strange chemical taste that reminded Seb of chlorine. The sooner he found a bar, the better.

The room had just one small window. A square pane of glass, it had a frosting over it from salt build-up. Seb listened to the harsh wind crash into it. Other than letting the light in, the window served very little purpose. Positioned too high up to see out of comfortably, the salt layer would have prevented Seb from seeing anything even if he were tall enough.

The receptionist might have said he had no hope of finding a job, but he had to try. He had no other alternatives if he wanted off the island. Besides, three hundred credits wouldn't last long.

***

"What do you want?" the large creature asked Seb.

Stood in front of the yellow-skinned being, Seb stared straight into her one eye and didn't reply. For a short while, the pair glared at one another, and Seb's heart pounded. After a deep breath, Seb said, "Do you have any work on your ship?"

With a hand on her holstered blaster, the monster scowled at Seb. "Even if I did have a job, which I don't, what makes you think I'd employ a human? Go away."

Having been on the end of such bluntness all day, Seb's pulse sped up and heat rushed through his cheeks. As he stepped closer, his world slowed down and the creature's throat became more prominent in Seb's vision. The waxy reek of the monster filled Seb's nostrils, and he clenched his jaw as he said, "You don't have to talk to me like that, you know."

The large being drew deep breaths that lifted her entire frame, and when she spoke, her words dragged because of Seb's slowed-down perspective. "I suggest you learn how to talk to others, little man. You upset the wrong beings around here and you're not likely to walk away from it."

In the stillness of slow motion, Seb's pulse kicked through him like a wet bass drum, and the creature's throat remained prominent to him. In only a few hours of walking the spaceport, Seb had been insulted, disrespected, and drained by every being he spoke to. Maybe he needed to try a different approach and talk to the space pirates in a language they understood. If he knocked one out, then maybe the others wouldn't be so rude to him when he did it all again tomorrow.

The back of the creature's ship hung open, and when Seb saw what appeared to be a male and children of the same species as the ship's captain, he stepped back a pace. The world returned to normal speed and Seb shook his head. No way could he attack someone in front of their family. The creature before him continued to stare fury at Seb, ground her jaw, and pulled her broad shoulders back. She didn't want trouble—Seb had been in enough fights to see that—but she wouldn't back down if he challenged her.

As Seb stroked his dad's necklace, his fury settled and he stepped back another pace. "Thanks anyway."

The creature didn't reply.

Seb walked away, squinting against the bright glare of Aloo's reflected sun.

***

Despite the almost blinding shine from the sea, Seb breathed more easily, relieved to be away from the gloomy docking area. It had been so crowded with ships that much of the sunshine—

and somewhat fresh air—was prevented from getting through. Drained from a morning of rejection and derision, Seb lifted his chin and began steeling himself for tomorrow. With a queue of ships in the sky above, there would no doubt be different opportunities when they docked. He could try all over again then.

Aloo didn't have much to it beyond the spaceport. A few market stalls that sold all kinds of foods and clothing, it also had what looked like one bar and a couple of restaurants. A small residential area sat farther back with about one hundred houses and lots of alleyways. Like on Danu, Aloo had been designed with surrounding buildings to act as windbreaks. Even with that, the salty wind still came at Seb like an onslaught of razor blades.

Any kind of subservience sat awkwardly with Seb, but he walked around Aloo with his head dipped to avoid eye contact with any other species. Aloo was a lawless pit of a place; Seb could handle the aggro if it came his way, but he didn't need to look for it.

***

None of the market vendors had any job vacancies, especially not for humans. With most of the city searched and on the end of unanimous rejection, Seb stopped dead when he heard the roar of a large crowd to his right. Hearing hisses, screams, laughter, and shouts, Seb stepped closer to the narrow passageway that it came from.

Although darker than the rest of the city, the alley still stood bright in the strong sun.

The sound lifted the hairs on the back of Seb's neck and his heart raced. He knew that sound. He'd recognise it from a mile away. The judgement from his dead father weighted his limbs, but not enough to stop Seb from stepping into the area.

The closer Seb got to the sound, the harder his heart beat. Dryness spread through his mouth and he swallowed against it, but it neither satiated his thirst nor calmed his excitement.

Butterflies danced in Seb's stomach when he rounded the corner and saw it. A structure bigger than any ship he'd seen docked that day, the building sat at the edge of the city. It looked like a huge stone silo, and the glistening ocean behind it threw a halo of light over the massive structure. They might have looked different on every planet, but they still had something universal about them. Seb smiled. Once you knew one fighting pit, you knew them all.

Chapter Eleven

The sound of the crowd set Seb's skin alight with gooseflesh when he walked through the huge archway into the fighting pit. Along with the reek of blood and sweat, the air sparked with excitement. His stomach tensed. The sport of a duel. The potential to win big. Although, just how big he couldn't tell; he'd never been to a fighting pit this large before.

A flight of stairs led up the back of the seating area. After Seb had climbed them, he looked around the place. It appeared to be a sell-out crowd. No wonder the spaceport had been so quiet when he'd walked around it.

The seats encircled a ring in the middle, which had a couple of lizard-like creatures cleaning it up for what must be the next fight. As the long, green beings—easily as tall as Seb should they stand on their hind legs—stalked around the ring, they used their elongated tails to sweep the floor. Teeth, flesh, and other body parts littered the hard and stained ground.

The anticipation hung so heavy in the air it damn near choked Seb as he made his way to a seat in the back row and dropped down into it. All of the seating area looked similar.

Round benches formed rings around the fighting space in the middle, each one positioned higher than the one in front of it so everyone had a view of the battle.

On one side, however, several rows of benches had been broken up by a box of some sort. A large, cushioned sofa sat in the box with a creature in a suit perched on it. At around ten feet tall, the creature had a neck as wide as its head, and its entire face pointed into a nose covered in scars. A wide mouth was filled with small razor-sharp teeth; the creature also had onyx eyes to complement its devilish grin. No one looked its way other than the bookies that walked in its direction and handed over what seemed to be credits. The suited beast clearly ran the place.

Silence fell around the pit as one of the lizard-like creatures stood up and faced the crowd. The creature drank it in for a moment as it spun on the spot before it said, "Thank you all for coming. The warm-up fight was entertaining, but we're sure you've all come for the main event. So, without further ado, can I have some noise for Aloo's fighting champion."

It lit a spark to the already charged atmosphere and the crowd exploded to life.

"Our longest-standing champion ever; she's a warrior from the great Arkint tribe, the bloodthirsty creatures that eat their mates once they've been impregnated by them, the one, the only, Mathusaaaaaaaaaaaaaa."

Although Seb expected the excitement to rise another level, the place fell into silence. A door opened in the wall that surrounded the ring and a bright light shone through it. A second later, the bench Seb sat on shook with a large bass *boom* that ran through the pit. Another *boom*, louder than the one before it. Then another.

The bright light diminished as it got blocked out, and the booms hit louder against the ground. A second later, Seb lost his breath when the biggest warrior he'd ever seen ran in, her heavy footsteps shaking the entire place. The fight announcer had introduced her as female; otherwise, Seb wouldn't have been able to tell. With legs thicker than Seb's entire body, and arms equally as large, the huge monster roared so loud it vibrated against Seb's chest and unsettled the rhythm of his heart.

The warrior then lifted her arms as a spotlight shone down on her. Pink-skinned, she had red eyes so close together Seb couldn't see the gap between them. Her hide looked as thick as leather. She had hair like ropes, and the smell of rotten meat filled the entire place at her entrance. When Seb looked over at the large suited creature in the box, he saw someone hand it a cup, which it slipped over its pointed nose—obviously to mask the stench.

As the champion paced around the ring, she stared up at the audience, and the commentator spoke. "Four hundred and sixty-two days since Mathusa first stepped into this ring. The purse for beating her now stands at three thousand credits. That'll keep you going on Aloo for a year at least. Who fancies it?"

So sure of herself, Mathusa continued to watch the crowd and roared again.

The muscles in Seb's legs twitched with the need to stand. It didn't matter who he went against, he'd find their weak spot and put them down. Three thousand credits would solve a lot of problems. He'd promised his dad he wouldn't fight again—especially not for money—but three thousand credits …

Before Seb could think on it any further, a creature stood up in the front row and the pit fell silent. Only slightly smaller than Mathusa, the creature had a large head with huge jaws and jagged teeth. It had four legs and two massive arms. A blow from any one of those appendages looked like they could win the fight.

"All righty then," the commentator called out, "we have ourselves a challenger." When he glanced up at the suited creature in the box, it nodded its approval.

While the challenger removed its leather waistcoat, the commentator addressed the crowd. "Now, as you all know, this is Aloo. We have no laws here, so we have no rules in the fighting pit. Anything goes, and the fight is often to the death."

A mixture of excitement and fear balled in Seb's stomach. He should be down there collecting the purse.

The challenger jumped down into the ring, and the commentator pointed to one side to show him where to go. Mathusa stood opposite him, her lip lifted in a snarl, her fists opening and closing as they hung down by her sides.

The commentator looked from the challenger to the champion. "Okay, I'm going to leave the ring now. When you hear the bell, the fight starts. Whoever's left standing wins. You understand?"

Although the challenger had watched the commentator for the entire time and nodded his agreement, Mathusa said nothing as she stared at her opponent.

The commentator left the ring. The only sound in the entire

place came from Mathusa's heavy breaths as she rocked with her respiration and stared at the monster opposite her.

***

The atmosphere wound so tight it could snap as everyone in the pit waited for the bell to ring, the challenger paced back and forth with his eyes on Mathusa. Mathusa remained dead still and breathed, almost as if in meditation.

The bell sounded as a loud clattering ring that sparked Mathusa to life. She charged straight at the four-legged creature opposite her.

The challenger rose up on his rear legs and kicked the onrushing champion. Both hooves caught Mathusa in the chest, and the large warrior stumbled backwards and fell with a loud *Ooof.*

A quick glance at the box and Seb saw the creature in the suit jump to its feet. This clearly didn't happen often.

Before Mathusa could get up, the challenger ran over to her and played a drumbeat against her face with his two front hooves. The champ looked like she could go down.

Then she caught one of his feet with one of her large hands; then the other. Although the challenger kicked and twisted, he couldn't get free from Mathusa's tough grip. Like a fly caught in a web, the challenger shook with panic, seemingly powerless to escape.

A broad grin stretched across Mathusa's wide face and she slowly got to her feet. As she stood up, she pulled the challenger with her, and the pit fell silent once again.

With one of her large fists clamped over each of the

challenger's feet, Mathusa lifted the creature from the ground as if its considerable weight meant nothing to her.

The challenger seemed to be caught like a fish on a line, and Mathusa held him far enough away from her that his flailing arms and legs came nowhere near making contact.

When her already wide grin stretched into a sadistic grimace, Seb's stomach tightened.

A second later, the ripping sound of breaking bones cracked through the pit from where Mathusa had taken the front feet of the challenger and pulled them apart so fast, it tore the creature's chest wide open.

A hot copper reek filled the air, and Mathusa laughed as she bathed in the black blood of her opponent.

For the next few seconds, she stood with the dead creature limp in her grip. When she let him go, the creature crashed down to the ground with a heavy *thud* as if its flaccid body had never been animated. It lay there like a bag of rocks, just a sack of muscle and bone.

The crowd erupted into cheers and whoops. With the same stony expression that had crushed her face for the entire time she'd been in the ring, Mathusa looked around at the gathered spectators. A sneer of contempt arched her lip and she grunted before she walked toward the gap that had opened up in the pit wall again.

Sure, Mathusa looked like she could fight. A brute, she could tear most opponents apart just like Seb had witnessed, but most opponents didn't have Seb's fighting skills. Three thousand credits would certainly help his current predicament, but the promise he'd made to his dad echoed in his mind. He'd already broken that promise once; no way could he break it another time. There had to be a better way to get the funds he needed.

A more honest way.

As she disappeared, Seb got to his feet. He could beat her if he wanted to. Size didn't matter when you had his skills. But he couldn't fight. He'd promised. With a shake of his head, Seb turned his back on the fighting pit and left.

Chapter Twelve

Despite the bright glare from the ocean, the mood in Aloo failed to lift. Everyone walked around with a permanent scowl as they dipped their heads into the salty wind. Any attempt to commune with a stranger resulted in an angry glare or worse. Mistrust ran high in Aloo, and it seemed that most beings had something to hide, especially when they came into contact with a human.

As Seb walked past the lines of ships docked and refuelling, he saw that every one of them, without fail, had a guard by the cargo hold. Each guard had a blaster of one description or another, and each guard looked more than prepared to use the weapons they wore. Would working for any one of this lot be any more reputable than fighting in the pit?

In the middle of what seemed to be a particularly busy area for the ships to dock stood food stalls where different merchants sold different delicacies. The smell of spices made Seb's mouth water, and his stomach rumbled. His wage wouldn't last long, but he needed to spend some of it on food. He had drinkable water back at his hotel, and although it tasted like crap, he could get by on it until he could afford the bottled stuff.

Despite the fierce winds, when Seb got closer to the counters, the smell of spices and oils increased tenfold. A quick scan of the prices and he walked over to the cheapest of the four. Cheaper by a long shot, he'd have to eat there. Until he got a job, he couldn't fritter his credits away.

The vendor smiled at Seb as he approached. At least, it looked like a smile. With such a small mouth and black eyes, the creature about to serve him didn't look like it had smiling in its repertoire. When the creature blinked, its eyelids met in the middle as a vertical slit. At about four feet tall, it looked like one of the sea slugs it had laid out on the counter in front of it—minus the slime.

"Um, hi," Seb said.

The creature dipped a short and sharp nod at him.

As Seb looked down at the trays of slugs, the beginnings of a heave rose up in his throat. "So this is all you have? Sea slugs?"

The creature nodded again, slightly less patient for the question.

"And I can eat them, can I?"

On the same sign that displayed the cheap price of the slugs sat several images. Each one had a picture of a species on it, and they'd either been surrounded by a red circle with a stripe through it, or they had a green tick next to them. When Seb saw the human image and the large green tick next to it, his entire being sank. He had to save money and he had no excuse not to eat here.

Seb handed over his credit card. A quick check of the sign again for the prices, and he said, "Just a quarter of a slug, please."

Unlike the slugs on the tray, the vendor had arms. They might have been small and had shrivelled hands on the ends of them, but they seemed to work just fine. It took Seb's credit card, processed it, and passed it back to him. When it lifted a huge meat cleaver, longer than its own little arms, the sun caught the blade and glistened off both the metal and the slug slime and guts that coated it. Swirls of green and red slug innards shone on the hefty cleaver. No matter how many times Seb swallowed, he couldn't relieve the nausea in his guts.

The blade cut through the slug with a *whomp* that removed a sizeable chunk from the thing. The vendor then lifted the floppy slab of slimy meat and passed it to Seb on a napkin.

The goo instantly soaked through to Seb's hand. The cold dampness of it against his palm sent his skin into a writhing spasm. He gulped several times as he looked down at it. "Hey," he said and looked back up at the vendor and smiled, "I don't suppose you have any work going, do you?"

Although the vendor might have struggled with joy, it seemed to have a good handle on contempt as it screwed its face up at Seb, clearly disgusted by his suggestion.

Deflated from both the prospect of his lunch and yet another rejection, Seb walked away.

Once several paces from the vendors, the wind battering him and stinging his skin, Seb lifted the slug to his mouth. As he opened wide, he caught the first reek of the creature. Somewhere between rotting food and sewage, the strong stench choked Seb momentarily. But he wouldn't be beaten by it. He needed to eat and couldn't afford to let his meal go to waste.

Another deep breath and Seb opened wide. When the strong

wind rushed into his mouth, Seb tasted the salt in the air. With his eyes closed, he bit a large chunk of slug away from the squishy and slimy lump in his hand.

The meat gave way to Seb's bite like jelly and damn near disintegrated as he chewed on it. A strange metallic taste rode the slime down his throat, and Seb nearly stopped. But the need for sustenance overrode his disgust, and the vendor had said the food would be edible for humans.

Seb battled his body's reluctance. He chewed with a weakened jaw and gulped against his need to vomit. The longer Seb ate, the more the taste changed. Once metallic, it now took on a strong and sour flavour. The rich taste ran a convulsion down Seb's neck, and his guts flipped as if to reject it before it had entered his body.

With further mastication, the slug turned into sludge in Seb's mouth. It felt like swilling snot, and after another hesitant gulp, Seb spat the rest out. When he dropped the part he hadn't eaten, the meat hit the ground with a wet *squelch* and lay quivering on the pavement like a beached jellyfish. The napkin caught in the wind and flew away from him like a greasy gull.

Seb watched it for a second or two longer before he looked up at the vendor who'd refused him work, shook his head at him, and walked away. It didn't matter how hungry he felt, he'd have to spend more credits to get a decent meal.

Chapter Thirteen

It didn't matter that Seb had found some other food—a cooked and spiced rodent from a planet he'd never heard of, its chewy meat tasted a lot like chicken—he couldn't banish the experience of eating the slug from his mind.

Even after he'd walked down the spaceport one more time, looking for work, and met aggressive rejection after rejection, nothing affected him quite as much as his attempted lunch had. The slimy memory would stay with him for a long time. He could still taste the metallic goo in his throat.

At the end of a row of cargo ships, Seb returned to the bar he'd seen when he first walked the length of the spaceport. Maybe the only one in Aloo—he certainly hadn't seen any others—he walked up to the ramshackle premises. It stood detached from the other buildings around it. Within staggering distance from the fighting pit, it no doubt saw a lot of rowdy customers.

It had been a long day and Seb needed a drink. He could spend a few credits relaxing. He'd find a way to make the money he needed, but for now, he had to switch off.

When Seb stepped into the bar, the large place fell quiet. As one of the early empires in the galaxy, the human race did some abhorrent things in its quest to colonise other worlds. Often met with open hostility wherever he went, Seb still hadn't gotten used to the way an entire room could turn to look at him like it did at that moment.

A bar on one side ran the length of the room—at least fifteen metres long. A quick check for the most shadowed space along the dark wooden counter, and Seb saw it unoccupied. He walked over and took his place there.

A few seconds later, the bartender—a spindly chartreuse-skinned creature with loose limbs that looked like a giant stick insect—walked over to Seb, stopped in front of him, and stared at him with its lime-green eyes.

When it said nothing, Seb laughed to himself. "Um ... can I have a drink, please?"

The silence in the place hung thicker than before and the barman continued to stare at Seb. After a deep breath, Seb raised an eyebrow at the creature—calm in the face of its hostility—and he stared back. Although his species might have been responsible for pain and suffering, he had no say in it and wouldn't be bullied because of it. "I said—"

"I heard what you said."

Agitation snapped through Seb and his heart rate increased. Seb straightened his back. "Well, get me a drink, then, bar keep."

"Why should we serve your kind here?"

"Because I'm paying. My credits work just like all of the others' credits do. So get me a drink."

Pains streaked up the side of Seb's face as he ground his jaw and refused to break eye contact with the creature in front of him.

The bartender finally placed a shot glass in front of Seb and filled it with a brown spirit.

Seb knocked the drink back, the liquid setting fire to his throat and then burning when it settled in his gut a few seconds later. As much as he wanted to avoid it, Seb flinched at the strong taste of the drink before he looked back at the bartender. "Another."

Before the bartender served a second drink, he held his hand out for Seb's credit card. After he'd swiped the card to claim the credits, he gave Seb another drink. "I'd take that one a bit easier if I were you. As a human in a new place, it may be sensible to keep your wits about you."

***

Seb took the bartender's advice and sipped the fiery liquid he'd been given. With a slight light-headedness from the first drink, he needed to remain vigilant. From the way the patrons stared at him, it looked like any one of them would love an excuse to fight him.

Before Seb took another sip of his drink, the bar fell quiet again. He'd thought he'd get a couple in before the other beings in the bar turned on him. After a deep breath and exhale, Seb closed his eyes before he shifted around. If he had to fight, he would. If his life rested on it, his promise to his dad would go out the window.

But the silence hadn't happened because of him. Instead, he

saw Mathusa—complete with about ten hangers-on—stride into the bar. Seb pulled into what shadow he had in the corner and watched the circus that surrounded the large fighter.

As she reached the other end of the bar to Seb, Mathusa slammed her fists down on it so hard Seb's shot glass jumped, and a small amount of the liquid spilled onto the dark varnished wood.

"Drinks for everyone, please, bartender."

With no trace of the hostility the bartender had aimed at Seb, he nodded at Mathusa, lined up glasses on the bar—his long limbs dragging the containers over from anywhere and everywhere—and began filling them so fast his arms turned into a blur.

Every creature in the bar got to their feet to wait in line for Mathusa to hand out the drinks.

Still covered in the dark blood of the creature she'd fought in the pit, Mathusa sniffed her clothes and released a maniacal shriek. "Poor thing. It didn't know what hit it when it stepped into the ring with me."

The very edges of Seb's consciousness slowed down as he looked at the brute in the bar, but he shook it off. There would be no fighting today.

"Raise your hands if you came to the fight."

Most of the bar had formed as a circle of sycophants around Mathusa, and nearly every one of them raised their hands.

With both hands resting on her ample stomach as if to contain her mirth, Mathusa arched her back, stared up at the ceiling, and laughed with all her might. Seb felt the bass of it in his chest. "I ripped it wide open. I didn't need to kill it, I could have knocked it out easily, but creatures need to learn. What happens when they step into the ring with the mighty Mathusa?" The huge brute paused, looked at those around her, and cupped a hand to her ear.

The sound of at least thirty voices said in unison, "They get finished."

Mathusa and the gathered crowd laughed as one. Some clearly forced their reaction, their eyes giving away the derision they felt for the Arkint warrior. Clearly in awe of her, some, however, meant it,

Visibly roused by the attention, Mathusa stepped up onto a table. Most tables would have groaned beneath her huge weight, but most bars had reinforced furniture. Always a place for violence, any bar owner with a brain made sure they furnished it so it resembled a fighting pit. After all, they didn't need to worry about the decor because the booze brought the customers in. With both of her large pink arms raised aloft, Mathusa drew a deep breath and released a booming roar.

In the pit, much farther away than he currently sat, Seb had felt her mighty roar push against him. Now he sat much closer, the deep rumble shook his bones.

The bar cheered.

While stood on the table, Mathusa looked around until she made eye contact with Seb. She stopped and glared at him. She'd obviously seen he hadn't applauded. The place fell silent and Seb sank with a sigh. This didn't need to be happening now. He took a sip of his fiery drink and his face twisted involuntarily.

When Mathusa jumped down off the table, Seb's stool shook. Each heavy step slammed down against the hard floor.

The tension in the bar hung so heavy, it pressed against Seb's skin.

As Mathusa walked closer, not only did she bring her stench of rotten meat with her, but her large form blocked out the light in the bar. "You ain't laughing."

Everything slowed down, so Seb forced it away with a deep inhale. He didn't need it now because he wouldn't fight her, no matter how much she antagonised him. "I don't find you funny."

A collective gasp swirled around the room.

As Mathusa stared down at Seb with her hands on her hips, she tilted her head to one side. "Oh?"

"Look, I don't want any grief. I just don't find you funny is all."

"I'm afraid it's too late to avoid grief, you stinking human."

It always came back to that. A legacy left behind from his ancestors, Seb had to pay the price for their murderous domination of the galaxy.

Instead of responding, Seb turned away from Mathusa and sipped his drink again.

"Well? What do you have to say?"

In one movement, Seb could jump to his feet and lay her out, but it would serve no purpose. If he ever were to fight this being, he'd make sure to do it in the pit, where he'd get paid for it.

"Look," Seb said, "I'm sorry I've offended you." He held his glass up. "Let me buy you a drink and we can forget about this, yeah?"

Mathusa knocked the glass from Seb's hand. The slow motion

returned and Seb watched the glass spin through the air in an arc that ended with a *splash* of breaking glass. With his pulse as a swollen and slow throb in his ears, he looked at the monster in front of him. The spot on her temples stood out prominently. One whack and she wouldn't know what had hit her.

As Seb pulled back from his fighting state, he focused on the room around him again and smiled at Mathusa. "I'll take it that you don't want a drink, then, shall I?"

The pair stared at one another and neither spoke.

Mathusa finally broke the stand-off. "I *hate* humans."

Seb smiled at her again and stared straight into her blood-red eyes. "So do I."

Chapter Fourteen

Once Mathusa had walked far enough away from him, Seb called the bartender over. The long green creature had kept his distance for the entire time Seb had spoken to Mathusa. Seb couldn't blame him for that. If it kicked off, Mathusa would crack most creatures' skulls, so why would they put themselves in the firing line?

Unable to suppress his broad smile because he'd finally avoided a fight, Seb stroked his dad's silver necklace. "Can I get another glass, please?"

The bartender looked at Seb, and his lime-green eyes narrowed as if trying to assess his sanity. Not that Seb could blame him for that. No one knew of Seb's abilities, so to see his behaviour around Mathusa—especially with the obvious size difference between them—would doubtlessly leave beings questioning his mental state.

By the time the bartender had brought another glass over and poured Seb another drink, Mathusa had joined her tribe. The second she stepped into their fold, the large warrior regaled them with her fight stories all over again. She'd no doubt told each one a thousand times already, and by the looks of the glazed eyes, fixed smiles, and vacant expressions that surrounded her, no one wanted to point that out. When she glanced over, Seb smiled and raised his drink. The bartender jumped a couple of paces away from him so as to distance himself from Seb's behaviour once again. Mathusa ignored Seb and returned to the beings who adored her. As Seb watched her, he took a sip of the fiery brown spirit in his glass. An involuntary spasm twisted through him as the liquid burned on its way down.

Before Seb could antagonise Mathusa again, a short creature walked into the bar and hopped up onto the stool next to him. For all intents and purposes, she looked human, except she stood no more than about three and a half feet tall. A tiny being, she wore glasses that had been fixed with tape, and had her black hair styled in a bob so sharp it could cut through paper.

When she looked over at Seb, he flinched. Magnified by her glasses, her large purple eyes drank him in. The small creature threw him a wonky smile before she turned to the bartender. The fingers on her hand stretched surprisingly long, easily twice the length of Seb's. She held one of them up to the bartender and said, "One shot, please."

For the first time since he'd been in the spaceport, Seb had found a being he could understand without a translator chip. When she spoke, her mouth formed the words that Seb heard.

Before the bartender could put her shot down on the long bar, the small creature took the shot glass from his grip and knocked it back. The *crack* as she slammed the empty vessel down called the attention of Mathusa, who broke away from her story and stared over. The small creature seemed oblivious to the attention she'd attracted.

After a glance first at his latest customer, Seb, and then Mathusa, the bartender shrugged and filled her glass again.

The small girl moved so quickly when she snapped the glass up, drank it, and slammed it down again, Seb barely saw it. The *crack* of the glass hitting the bar called through the crowded space for a second time.

As the girl wiped her mouth with the back of her hand, her eyes widened and she said, "Another."

Although he tilted the bottle to pour her another one, the bartender stopped and looked at her. "How do you intend on paying for this?"

The wonky grin returned to the creature's face, and she winced like she already knew what the reaction would be. "Credit?"

Seb couldn't stifle his laugh at the bartender's reaction. When the angry creature looked at him, indignant at his response, Seb leaned in the girl's direction. "You're lucky you got two. He asked me for payment after my first one. You must look more trustworthy than I do."

All the while, the bartender rocked with heavy breaths and stared in fury at the pair.

At that moment, Mathusa broke away from her storytelling and looked across. The floor shook with her heavy steps as she walked over. She glared down at the small, and now slightly intoxicated, creature that had made herself two drinks in debt. No bigger than Mathusa's forearm, the girl looked up at her and giggled. Seb couldn't fight his own smile.

"What's going on here?" Mathusa asked.

"She can't pay her bill," the bartender responded.

Before Mathusa could say anything else, Seb said, "It's fine. I'm buying these drinks for her."

The small creature fixed Seb with her warm and wonky grin. "You will?"

"Yeah."

Despite the resolution, Mathusa continued to loom over the small girl. It seemed utterly pointless to intimidate someone so tiny. Heat flushed Seb's cheeks as he watched the bully and said, "We've sorted it now, thanks."

The red in Mathusa's eyes glowed like embers when she turned her focus back on Seb.

"Tell her," Seb said to the bartender without breaking eye contact with Mathusa. "I have the credits."

Mathusa looked at the bartender, who'd lost his rage in the face of hers. After he gulped, the bartender nodded at her.

Mathusa grunted and walked off, her footfalls the only sound in the packed bar.

When Mathusa had reached the other side of the bar again, the bartender held the bottle up in Seb's direction. Seb nodded and he filled the girl's glass. Unfazed by Mathusa, the small girl raised her drink at Seb. "Thank you."

Seb nodded again.

"I'm Sparks, by the way."

"I'm Seb. Nice to meet you."

"You too, wanna sit in a booth away from those degenerates over there?" She said it so loud half of the degenerates looked over.

The girl had spirit. Another laugh and Seb said, "Sure."

Chapter Fifteen

Although Sparks hadn't been wrong to call the space they currently sat in a booth, it didn't resemble what Seb would typically expect a booth to be. A near circular seated area, it had privacy, but it had none of the comfort Seb would assume it to have. A hard wooden bench with a hard, high back made it instantly uncomfortable to sit in. The angle of the back in relation to the seat forced Seb to lean forward slightly. The table in the middle had three legs and a stump where the fourth leg should have been, making it damn near impossible to put anything on it without losing it to the floor. The space reeked of dust and neglect.

With both of his shot glasses in his hands, Seb looked over at Sparks, who mirrored his posture. After these four shots, he wouldn't buy any more. He'd already spent a third of his credits on booze that day.

With a raised glass, he nodded at Sparks and knocked the drink back. Sparks did the same, hitting one shot after the other before she slammed down two empty glasses on the table. The two sharp cracks snapped through the busy bar and Sparks shouted, "Woooooeeeeeeeeeee," as she rocked back in her seat. After a glance at her onlookers, Sparks shouted again, "Woooooooooooo." The girl really didn't care who she upset. A second later, both of her glasses slipped from the wonky table and smashed against the hard floor.

Although she had quieted down, Sparks looked across the room and held the glare of those who stared at her.

Seb laughed. "You've got some spirit."

"For someone who's only three and a half feet, you mean?"

No way would Seb be dragged into that. As he looked into the accusation in her eyes, he shrugged. "You look young. How old are you?"

"Twenty-six."

"Twenty-six?"

"Is there an echo in here?"

Seb laughed. "Like I said, you have some spirit."

"I find you have to be able to hold your own in places like this. Especially when you look like I do."

It might have been considered rude, but Sparks didn't seem like the kind of girl to get hung up on etiquette, so Seb said, "Where are you from?"

"I'm from all over. I don't have a home. Although, that's not what you mean, is it?"

The intensity of her purple glare bored into Seb again, and he shrugged.

"I'm Katan."

When Seb said nothing, Sparks rolled her eyes. "No one's ever heard of us. We're a planet at the arse end of the galaxy that has nothing to offer other than eels."

"Eels?"

"Yep. Our planet—Katanish—isn't quite as wet as this, but we have a lot of water. It makes it a perfect breeding ground for eels. We catch them and ship them around the galaxy. They're considered to be quite a delicacy, but when you eat them every day, they get boring very quickly."

Before Seb could say anything, Sparks continued. "We're an academic race." After she looked down at herself, she laughed. "We'd hardly be a warrior race at this size, eh?"

As Sparks pushed her large glasses up her nose, Seb smiled. "Well, I'm human," he said.

"I know you're human. *Everyone* knows who humans are." When she lifted her glasses away from her face to look at Seb, her large purple eyes remained the same size rather than the magnification that Seb had previously thought them to be. "Quite a legacy you lot have left behind."

A shake of his head and Seb said, "Yeah, don't remind me. And please, don't judge me on the actions of my species. Our government made decisions that nobody supported, and the next thing we knew, we were at war with the galaxy. I'm not sure we'll ever live it down."

"Fortunately for you, you were pretty good at it; or rather, at least good enough to destroy the infrastructures of other planets so you could go in and take their resources. After you lot have broken somewhere, it stays broke—from what I hear, anyway. Who would visit a place after it had been ravaged by humans?"

A heavy sigh and Seb shook his head. "As a species, we're the ultimate parasite."

After he'd knocked back his next shot, light-headed from the booze and with his mouth aflame, Seb spoke with a slight slur to his words. "So what are you doing in this armpit of a place?"

"Just passing through," Sparks said. "This ain't the kind of place you want to stay in, is it?"

"Although," Seb said, "it also seems like it's quite a hard place to leave if you don't already have a ride out of here. I'm struggling to find the money or the transport to get me off this cursed planet."

Silence hung between the pair and Seb looked around the bar—mostly at Mathusa—while he stroked his dad's necklace. The large warrior clung on to a tankard of ale and, if anything, grew louder in her storytelling than before. Those around her continued to inflate her ego as they laughed and shouted along with her.

"I like that."

"Huh," Seb said when he turned back to Sparks.

Wide purple orbs locked on Seb's neck. "Your necklace. I like your necklace."

"Oh, thanks. It was my dad's."

Silence engulfed the pair again. Seb didn't need to explain about his dad, Sparks got it. Besides, who told a virtual stranger about the deaths in their family? Next, he'd be talking about the itchy rash on his right buttock. The sudden attention to his rash made Seb desperate to scratch it. Instead, he shifted from side to side so the hard bench could do the job for him.

When Sparks pulled out a tiny computer, Seb nodded down at it. "What's that?"

The wonky grin returned to Sparks' face, and she looked over at the bartender.

A glance at the long, green creature showed Seb he'd pulled his blasters down from the side and had them resting on the dark wooden bar. Mathusa and her crowd had grown louder, and he now watched the place, tense as if ready to use them.

Several quick taps lit the computer's screen up. Sparks' fingers moved so fast over the device, they turned into a blur. Once she'd finished, she looked up, an impish glee in her purple stare, and she said, "Come on, let's go."

Whatever she had planned, Seb knew he should leave with her at that point. The mood in the bar would probably take a turn for the worse very soon.

As they exited the booth, the bartender looked over at them, a heavy frown on his face. Sparks made the shape of a gun with her long fingers and pretended to shoot him while she clicked from the side of her mouth.

With his stare still fixed on them, the bartender reached out for his blasters and let out a low growl.

Seb laughed again as he placed his shot glasses on the bar. If size were anything to go by, Sparks should be the meekest and mildest creature in the galaxy.

Once outside in the spaceport, and a good fifty metres from the bar, Sparks removed her small computer again. A quick glance at Seb and her grin spread across her face before she pressed the screen.

A pop sounded out, and when Seb turned back to the bar, he saw all of their lights had blown. The grin on Sparks' face widened and Seb gasped. "You just did that?"

Sparks nodded. "I didn't like his attitude. That'll take him days to fix."

A half laugh and Seb shook his head. "You really are something, you know. Well"—he held his hand out to her—"it's been a pleasure meeting you, Sparks."

The small Katan stepped forward and threw her arms wide. When Seb kneeled down, she gripped him in a tight hug. "You too," she said. "And thank you for the drinks."

As he stepped back, slightly wonky from the booze, Seb nodded. "My pleasure." The pair backed away from one another. "See you around, Sparks."

Sparks saluted Seb, howled at the sky, and stumbled off in the opposite direction to him.

Chapter Sixteen

Seb woke with a warm glow like his head had been wrapped in a hot towel all night. A slight fuzz sat in his brain, numbing his thoughts and taking the edge off the low-level panic that had jangled through him since he'd been dropped off on Aloo. Drunk enough last night to have fun, but not so drunk he had to deal with a major hangover, Seb lay on his back and stared up at the cracks in his white ceiling.

As he woke up more, his surroundings came into focus. The wind outside howled and the moisture in the air battered the only window in the room like a wet fist knocking to get in. When Seb turned his head to look at the frosted glass, he let go of a weary sigh. At some point, he'd have to go out in that again.

The damp in the air had worked its way into the room and into Seb's sinuses. Tightness gripped his face from the moisture having been pulled from it and left his skin taut. The edges of his eyes, around his mouth, and beneath his nostrils buzzed as the sting of developing sores returned.

After he released a long groan, Seb covered his face with his hands. Cold from the room, they also reeked of salt. Maybe he could stay in bed today.

The previous evening flashed through Seb's mind. He'd insulted Mathusa, drunk more than he should have done, met Sparks, and paid for her to drink too. No way could he stay in bed today. With the amount of credits he'd spent in the bar, he'd have to find work much sooner now.

As Seb sat up in bed, his head thicker than he'd first anticipated, he stretched to the ceiling. He stood up on shaky legs and walked over to the grimy sink in the corner of the room. As he rested on the cold and dirty ceramic, Seb leaned forward and stared at his reflection. "You spent too many credits yesterday, you f—" The word left Seb and his jaw fell loose as he stared at his neck. "What the ...?"

Although his reflection made it pretty damn clear, Seb grabbed his neck anyway to feel his lack of necklace. He rushed over to the chair beside his bed. Not that he needed to. It didn't take a genius to work out what had happened. To confirm it, Seb lifted his trousers and plunged his hand into his now empty pocket. His necklace *and* wallet. Gone! The little ... And he'd bought her drinks too.

As Seb stood in his room, he clenched his fists, drew deep breaths, and rocked on the balls of his feet. He'd reached out to Sparks in an act of kindness and the little cargo rat had robbed him blind.

Despite the violence coiled within him, Seb continued to draw deep and slow breaths to calm himself down. A balled rage locked his muscles tight, but it wouldn't serve any purpose to smash the room up. Besides, he didn't have the credits to pay for the damage now anyway. Sparks, on the other hand, she'd feel the full force of his wrath when he got a hold of her.

Several more deep breaths and Seb put his clothes on.

***

Once he'd reached the bottom of the stairs and the hotel's foyer, Seb poked his head around the corner to see the receptionist behind the desk. With no one else in the place, she'd be bound to ask him for his rent that morning, and no way would he be able to sneak past someone with two heads.

As he hovered by the doorway, Seb scanned the place, chewed on his bottom lip, and tapped his right foot. When he saw the trigger for the fire alarm close by, he stared at it for a second. Too much more thought and he wouldn't do it, so Seb punched the glass at the front. He jumped when the shrill bell drove needles into his eardrums and echoed through his skull.

As he stepped out into the foyer, Seb looked at the receptionist and hooked a thumb over his shoulder behind him. "I think I smelled smoke back there."

The one eye on each of the receptionist's heads spread wide, and she nodded at him in stereo. "Thank you, thank you."

As the receptionist went one way, Seb rushed for the exit. At some point he'd have to face up to the fact that he had no money left, but if he could prolong it for as long as possible …

The sharp wind smashed into Seb when he stepped outside, and the points on his face that stung now burned as the salt corroded his skin. He could feel the edges of the sore spots spread with every passing second. He wasn't built for this environment. With his head dipped against the elements, Seb marched off toward the bar he'd been in the previous evening.

***

As Seb stepped into the dark bar, he looked around the large space. It seemed better for the lack of clientele—especially that oaf Mathusa. The barman had his back to the room as he cleaned the shelves. Seb cleared his throat and walked toward him.

When the long, green barman spun around, he stared at Seb, his bloodshot eyes a sign that he hadn't slept all night. His already heavy frown deepened and he pointed a stick-like finger at him. "You."

"Me?"

The barman pulled out one of his blasters and aimed it at Seb. "You were with that little rat yesterday. Where is she?"

As Seb focused on the barman's shaking hand, he drew a deep breath to settle his nerves. "I was hoping *you'd* be able to tell me that. The little rodent stole my necklace and credit card."

Some of the tension left the bar owner and he lowered his blaster slightly. "She blew my electrics. I don't know how she did it, but I *know* it was her. I should have kicked her out the second she walked into the place."

"So you've not seen her?"

"If I'd seen her, she'd be pinned to the wall by now with a hole in her forehead."

"Damn it."

Without another word, Seb spun on his heel and left the bar.

***

The cold saline wind burned Seb's eyes when he stepped outside again and kept his head raised. With tears streaming down his face and a squint that encouraged the collection of salt at the edges of his eyes, he scanned for signs of Sparks. She might only be small, but when Seb caught up with her, he'd destroy the little vermin.

As Seb passed the cargo ships in the port, he looked at each one, searching the shadows of their docking bays. The guards that saw him stared back. Some drew their blasters and pointed them at Seb. Whatever they had on their ship must justify their aggression, but Seb didn't want to know.

He'd walked from one end of the docking bay to the other and saw no sign of Sparks. Despite the time he'd spent with her the previous evening, he had no idea where she was staying on Aloo. She wouldn't have told him the truth even if he'd asked, the devious little rat.

Once out of the docking bay, Seb walked down the alleyway that led to the fighting pit, with his hands dug into his pockets and his shoulders raised to his neck. The tight space funnelled the fierce wind and turned it into an intense blast of cold and wet salt. But Seb rode out the pain and pushed on. With most of the beings on Aloo in the pit the previous day, maybe Sparks would be in there now.

The sound of the commentator came out of the open-fronted building and ran up the alleyway towards Seb. "Whoever beats Mathusa will earn three *thousand* credits."

As Seb walked, he shook his head. He'd promised his dad. No matter how skint, there had to be another way. But three thousand credits …

Seb stared at the large pit, and the hairs lifted on the back of his neck to hear the roar of the crowd. A look at the clear, blue sky and Seb grabbed for his necklace, his fingers closing around empty air. He'd promised his dad.

Chapter Seventeen

If for no other reason than to get out of the sharp wind, Seb walked into the fighting pit. Although, he had plenty of other reasons to go in and he knew it. Like an addict presented with his vice, Seb couldn't resist the call of violence.

The guards watched Seb as he entered. They probably watched everyone who entered, but there seemed to be an edge to their glare reserved only for humans.

A smile at the closest security guard—a porcine creature with yellow eyes, orange skin, and an odour like a cesspool—and Seb glanced down at his blaster before he looked back up and winked at the thing. "My, my, that's a big piece you have there."

The side of the guard's face swelled and rested as it clenched its jaw. Despite the unease Seb felt in the guard's presence, the fighting pits were his church and he knew the moves well. It would take a lot for a guard to justify shooting a punter. Their own delicate ego and bad temper wouldn't wash with the big man in the suit who ran the place.

It took until Seb reached the top of the stairs at the very back of the pit before he escaped the guard's smell. Maybe the reek didn't vanish completely, but it certainly got lost to the stench of blood and sweat that Seb associated with the fighting pits. The heady funk of pain and victory swirled through Seb's senses and his head spun. Most people would have turned their nose up at the smell, but for Seb it had the aroma of home. In a world where he had no place, the reek of combat grounded him and calmed his nerves.

When the crowd erupted, Seb looked down to see Mathusa. The smug fighter strolled into the ring like she owned it and walked circles around it as she stared at the crowd like she'd fight every one of them at once. Three thousand credits would go a long way, especially now that he had nothing.

As the commentator introduced Mathusa, Seb searched the gathered crowd for a small Katan with broken glasses and large purple eyes. Maybe Sparks thought she could hide out in here. Maybe she'd come here to gamble Seb's money away. Just the thought of it lifted Seb's heart rate as he searched for the little snake. However, he couldn't see her.

When the crowd fell silent and they all sat down, Seb looked to see a creature had remained on its feet, ready to fight Mathusa. Everyone looked across at the suited man in the box for his approval. The emperor of this pit, he stared at the challenger: a tall, but slim creature that looked agile and fast. He then gave a thumbs-up and the crowd erupted into raucous approval.

The challenger rolled his shoulders as he made his way down to the ring with the roar of the crowd behind him. Those on the benches didn't necessarily support him, but they supported the fight. Touts sprang up from the seated masses and flitted around as they took bets.

One of the lizard creatures who swept the floor of the pit came over with a ladder, but the tall challenger ignored it and vaulted over the side down into the ring. He'd clearly meant to land with grace and agility, but he caught his foot on the way over and fell to the floor like a rock.

Even at the back of the pit, Seb heard the *crack* of the creature's leg as it landed awkwardly. The crowd drew a collective intake of breath and the challenger screamed and grabbed its shin. Every tout in the pit sat down and ignored the angry calls from those around them. All bets were off.

Seb saw the fight announcer glance at the pit's boss. The suited creature rolled his hand through the air to signal that the fight should go on.

"Beings of the galaxy," the fight announcer called out, "it looks like the challenger has picked up an injury. But once you agree to fight the mighty Mathusa, there's no backing out." The creature looked almost embarrassed when it said, "Let's see what the challenger can do with a broken leg."

With a grip still on its shin, the tall being with the broken leg shook its head. "No, no, no."

As the commentator backed out of the gap in the pit that Mathusa had entered through, he said, "Let the fight begin."

The gap closed off, shutting the fight announcer away, and a loud bell rang through the place.

The normally noisy crowd watched on in near silence. The main sound came from the challenger. "Please, I'll come back when I'm healed, but please don't make me fight now."

While most faces pointed toward the fight, Seb looked at the creature in the suit. Impossible to read, his dark eyes watched things unfold below with what seemed to be a cold detachment. Not that he could look any other way; his obsidian glare left little room for compassion.

Mathusa crossed the ring at a jog, and the seats that surrounded it shook. Three heavy steps and the fourth one came down on the challenger's head. The stomp ran through the pit like she'd dropped an atomic bomb.

Silence descended on the pit. Although Seb couldn't see the downed creature from where he sat, he saw the splattering of blood and brain matter that coated the walls of the ring. A stick of lit dynamite in the challenger's mouth would have made less of a mess.

With her huge arms raised, Mathusa spun on the spot. The crowd jumped up as one, and the large creature drank in the adoration as she continued to turn. She then roared so loud it shook Seb's vision.

To beat her would see Seb right for at least a year. Without thinking, Seb grabbed the space where his dad's necklace should be. After another quick scan of the rowdy spectators, he saw no sign of Sparks. As the rest of the crowd sat down, Seb turned to leave. He needed to get his dad's necklace back before he did anything else.

By the time Seb had reached the stairs at the back of the pit that led to the exit, the voice of the fight announcer echoed through the large space. "Our esteemed host, Moses Deloitte, has just upped the purse for anyone who wants to fight Mathusa. For this next fight, and this next fight only, the prize has been raised to four thousand credits."

Seb stopped and looked down at the crowd. Most of the

beings gasped, but none stood up. And why would they? They'd just seen a contender so utterly destroyed, it would hardly fill them with confidence to have a go themselves.

The pit had gone so quiet, Seb could hear the scuff of the fight announcer's feet as he turned circles in the middle, looking for someone to challenge Mathusa. "Anyone? Four thousand credits will make life a lot easier."

"So will staying alive," a large brute of a creature called out. All hair and claws, it sat close to the pit and shook its head at the announcer.

While the announcer tried to find a challenger, Mathusa limbered up behind him. A smug smile spread across her wide face as she looked at the crowd. Her superiority complex oozed from her. When she made eye contact with Seb, she stopped her surveillance and laughed. A full-bellied laugh, each bark of it went off like cannon fire.

It didn't take long for everyone in the pit to look up at Seb. The only person on his feet, Mathusa must have seen him as her next challenger. A laugh here and there, and then the entire pit burst into hysterics at the perceived challenge.

Heat flushed Seb's face when he looked around. Even the announcer laughed at him. The only being who didn't seem amused by the misunderstanding sat in the box in a suit. Instead, he stared at Seb. The beast's thoughts were impossible to read because of his dark visage.

Something inside of Seb snapped. He'd chosen to walk away, but by mocking him, Mathusa had just signed her fall from grace. With his attention still on the creature in the suit, Seb said, "All right then, I'll fight her."

Chapter Eighteen

Seb stared at Moses, and Moses stared straight back. Eyes as dark as the bloodstones on Danu, Seb searched them but found Moses impossible to read. Near silence descended on the huge pit. Even the fight announcer remained quiet.

With his heart in his throat, Seb waited. Now he'd made the choice, he wanted this fight. Hell, if Moses didn't give it to him, he'd go down there and take it. "If you're worried about my size," Seb said, his voice echoing across the quiet space, "then don't be. Trust me, I can hold my own."

The slightest twitch of a smile pulled on Moses' wide mouth and he tilted his head to one side.

After a glance down at Mathusa, Seb looked back at the creature in the suit. "You should be more worried about *her* than me."

The pit exploded into laughter. Even Moses smiled to reveal his mouth full of razor-sharp teeth. Despite his smile, his cold eyes still showed no sign of emotion. The glare of a psychopath. Not that psychopath meant anything to any species other than human; being a psychopath could be the highest achievement among Moses' race for all Seb knew.

Before Seb could say anything else, Moses smiled again, broader than before, and gave a thumbs-up. The crowd screamed so loud Seb had to clap his hands to his ears to shut out the pain of it.

With what felt like every pair of eyes on him, Seb walked from the back of the pit down to the ring in the centre. A long and lonely march, he felt the derision aimed at him from everyone in the place. How could such a slight human take on the mighty Mathusa?

Once he arrived at the pit, one of the lizard creatures pushed a ladder up for him to climb down.

"Make sure you don't slip," the announcer called out, and the pit filled with laughter again.

So calm, Seb had slowed his heart rate down to a resting pace. While he climbed down the ladder, three of the lizard creatures rushed around the ring to tidy up the mess left from the previous fight.

By the time Seb had descended the three metres into the ring, the creatures had cleaned the place. There remained no sign of Mathusa's destruction of yet another one of her challengers. Seb walked over to his side of the ring, turned around, and stared at Mathusa. Now he'd climbed down to her level, her foul stench of rotting meat smothered him.

Mathusa's breaths rolled inside her chest like thunder and vibrated through the ground. Huge arms and legs, she stretched them out as she paced back and forth while she maintained her focus on Seb. With red eyes too close together, she watched him with more malice than he'd seen from her before; the challenge from such a small being clearly got under her thick hide.

"Now, if we can have your attention," the announcer called, his voice echoing through the pit. "This is the big one. Never seen before, our gracious host, Moses Deloitte, is offering a four-thousand-credit purse to ..." The announcer looked at Seb.

"Seb Zodo," Seb said.

A shrug and the announcer laughed. "Not that it matters, he'll be mush within thirty seconds." The crowd giggled again. "But for the sake of consistency, let me introduce you to Seb Zodo."

The pit had been quiet when Seb awaited permission from Moses to step into the ring. Now it seemed like even the idea of noise had been sucked into a vacuum.

When the announcer cleared his throat, it went off like a gunshot. "And the champion, as you all know, the one, the only, Mathusaaaaaaaaaaa."

The gathered mass of creatures all jumped from their seats and screamed as loud as they had been quiet just seconds before. So loud, it made Seb's head spin. When he looked at Moses, he found the man staring straight at him. No expression on his face, the black eyes of the creature fixed Seb with something that could have been curiosity, but who knew?

As Seb waited for the crowd to calm down, he rolled his shoulders and bounced on the spot. Mathusa, easily three to four times his size, stared at him with contempt. When the sound in the place dropped quiet enough, she said, "Why are you here?"

Seb didn't reply; instead, he grinned at her and rocked from side to side in an attempt to loosen up.

Her voice rumbled when she asked again, louder this time,

"Why are you here? Tell me. You obviously can't beat me, so what do you want to achieve?"

"Quit talking, yeah?" A few of the onlookers gasped at Seb's words. "Just fight me and we'll see, shall we?"

The ugly Arkint warrior fixed her gaze on Seb for a few more seconds before she shrugged and then focused on the announcer.

A look from Seb to Mathusa, and the announcer backed out of the ring.

The calmest he'd been since he'd landed on Aloo, Seb watched the wall close back over before he refocused on Mathusa, her red eyes so close together they nearly touched in the middle.

The second the announcer shouted, "Fight!" Seb's world slipped into slow motion.

Despite Seb's perception of the world moving slower, Mathusa rushed forward like the wind and closed the space down in a flash. Thankfully, he didn't have to fight her at full speed. A wall of flesh and limbs, she landed the first blow. The connection hit Seb's jaw, snapped his face to the side, lifted him from his feet, and hurled him halfway across the ring like a rag doll.

With the copper taste of his own blood rushing down his throat, Seb lay on his back as Mathusa closed down on him once again. Each step shook the ground, and before Seb had recovered, the huge warrior woman loomed over him as she brought her large fist, easily the size of Seb's torso, crashing down toward him.

This time, Seb rolled to the side and she missed him. The impact ran a shock wave through the hard ground of the pit, and Seb bounced like a pea on a drum. As he scrambled to his feet, his legs wobbly from the first punch and his vision blurred, he drew a deep breath of her rotting stench and shook his head.

Mathusa came forward again and led with a punch that Seb ducked. She hit the wall above him and the top of it broke away. Before the huge concrete lump could land on him, Seb dived through Mathusa's legs.

Having shaken off the effects of the first punch, Seb jumped up and bounced on the balls of his feet as he waited for Mathusa's next move. The brute only knew one way: attack, attack, and attack. Sure enough, she came at him again, her mouth opened wide in a roar and her arms raised, ready to land another punch.

With the world around him in slow motion, Seb focused on Mathusa's temples. Either one would do; even a half-decent punch would knock her out.

As she came at him again, Seb ducked beneath her reach, dodged to the side, jumped up, and landed a punch square on her temple as she passed him.

Momentum carried Mathusa straight into the ring's wall, which she connected with head first before she fell into a heap. Seb kept his fists raised as he stared at the felled warrior, but when she didn't move, he lowered his guard and took in the stunned crowd.

The call of "Finish her" shook the walls of the place, so Seb walked over to her. Still out cold, he could end the bully's life. Maybe he'd be doing the galaxy a favour. But to kill her would be to stoop to her level. His mercy would do more damage than any physical blow ever could. So instead, Seb put his foot on her back like a proud hunter with a downed beast, and lifted his hands above his head. The crowd damn near deafened Seb with their celebration.

The voice of the fight announcer rang out as he came back through the gap in the walls. "Wow, wow, and wow. What can I say? After years of domination, the mighty Mathusa has been knocked out. But can I ask something?"

Seb shrugged.

"Why didn't you finish her? She always finishes her opponents."

At that moment, Seb addressed Moses rather than the announcer. "Do I need to finish her?"

Moses shook his head.

"Then that's why. Why kill someone when you don't have to? This is a sport. I needed the purse, so I fought her. I don't care whether she lives or dies, just about when I get paid." Another glance at Moses. "When do I get paid?"

The creature in the suit smiled, but he didn't reply.

"Don't worry," the fight announcer said, "we'll get you the credits, of that you can be certain. So tell me, how was it fighting her?"

Seb stared at the microphone the fight announcer had shoved in his face and then up at the crowd. Hundreds of expectant looks stared down at him, awaiting an answer. Sod them; they didn't deserve anything from Seb. Without another word, Seb spun on his heel and walked out of the ring.

Chapter Nineteen

Not only did Seb's face and limbs ache, but the hairs on his body ached too. If Mathusa had caught him one more time, she would have put his lights out for sure. As he lay on his back on his bed in his crappy hotel room, he looked at the streak of diluted light that came through the window and ran across the cracked ceiling. Even if he'd wanted to clean it, the salt probably wouldn't come off the pane anyway. From a cursory glance, it looked like the crusty white layer had fused to the glass and had now become a part of it—he wouldn't have had a great view out of it anyway. If he never saw a rolling sea again …

An abrupt knock snapped through the room and Seb looked at the door. He turned a little too quickly, which sent a sharp twinge up the back of his neck and into the base of his skull. With his hand wrapped around the pain, he winced as he said, "Come in."

The door opened and one of the lizards Seb had seen cleaning the ring floor stepped into the room. A buzz of anxiety pulled Seb's stomach tight.

The lizard nodded at Seb before it stood aside to let Moses

in. The large suited creature had to duck to enter. At easily ten feet tall, he had the kind of physique that could block out the sun. Once inside, Moses stood with a hunch so he didn't bash his head on the ceiling. It made him look even larger, and he glared at Seb through his dark eyes.

Wincing as he sat up, Seb breathed a relieved sigh when Moses held a hand up to him. "Don't get up." He then pulled a credit card from his top pocket. "I've come to deliver this to you. Well done in the fight today. I nearly didn't let you into the ring, you know."

When Seb gulped, he tasted the copper tang of his own blood. "Oh? Why's that?"

"Well, look at the size of you compared to Mathusa." He tapped one of his fat fingers against his temple. "I took my time in making my decision because I needed to work out if you had all of your marbles. I guess I made the right choice."

"Or the wrong one if you were hoping to keep Mathusa as the champion."

The dark eyes fixed on Seb and a cold expression pulled Moses' face taut. "I'm all for competition, Seb. Fighters come and go. That's the nature of the fighting pits."

A shrug ran electric pain through Seb's torso and he dragged a sharp intake of breath through his clenched teeth. "I guess it is."

After Moses had placed the credit card on the bedside table, he looked around the room. "You like staying here?"

"What do you think?"

Moses smiled, although the potential bite contained within his wide mouth held a warning, and Seb felt the ice creak and groan beneath him. "You may want to consider how you talk to me, boy."

The pair stared at one another in silence before Moses said again, "Do you like staying here?"

When Seb didn't respond, Moses shook his large and scarred head. "Didn't think so. How would you like to stay in a much more luxurious place than this?"

"That depends."

"On what?"

"On what I would have to do to get said luxurious accommodation."

Moses inhaled to speak, but Seb cut him off, "I'm not fighting again."

The large suited man tilted his head to one side. "But you'd make a killing … *I'd* make a killing. People who hadn't seen you fight would bet big against you. We'd clean up night after night."

"I'm not interested. I promised someone very dear to me that I wouldn't fight any more."

"So why did you fight today?"

"I needed the money. Someone robbed me and I can't find her to get back what she stole. I need to have enough credits to stay here while I track her down, and then I'm getting off this damn planet. I hate it here."

Moses' laugh seemed to shake the walls. He threw his head back and exposed his rows of razor-sharp teeth and thick pink tongue. With one snap, he could bite Seb's head clean off should he so desire.

The mirth left him and he fixed Seb with his dark stare again. "Are you sure you can't be persuaded?"

Seb shook his head.

"I understand." The large creature leaned toward Seb. He stank of fish. "Although, understand this; I haven't given up on the idea yet, and when I want something, I usually get it."

"Are you threatening me?"

A shake of his head and Moses linked his hands together in front of his chest while he smiled a predatory grin. "I'll see you around, Seb. And congratulations again on the fight."

Moses left the room first, followed by his lizard assistant. They didn't look back. When the lizard slammed Seb's door shut, silence filled the room. The aches somehow felt worse now than before. Seb dropped his head back against his wafer-thin pillow and closed his eyes. What had he gotten himself into?

Chapter Twenty

Seb walked down the spaceport, searching for Sparks. He looked at the sealed-off cargo holds of the many ships that pointed his way. The sharp and salty wind burned his eyes, stung the sores that spread across his skin, and damn near deafened him as he scanned the shadows for the rat. Once he found her, he'd take back what belonged to him and get the hell off Aloo.

As Seb walked, he made eye contact with every guard for every ship. From small to large, they spanned the rainbow in the colours of their skin. Some seemed a physical impossibility, yet there they stood, one leg and a top-heavy body, or a head so large, the neck shouldn't be able to carry it. Hostility emanated from every one of them, and every one of them had one weapon or another that they seemed more than willing to use. Blasters, all in different shapes and sizes, they wore them loud and proud.

Another strong breeze rattled into Seb and he pulled his coat tighter around himself. Despite the aches from his fight with Mathusa and the assault from the wind, he walked with a bounce in his step. The rush from the fighting pit remained with him. The burden of guilt he should have felt because he'd fought again had also been lifted from his shoulders. He had no choice but to fight the previous day. Even his dad, were he still alive, would have understood that. With no money and no hope, it was what he had to do—but not again.

Sleek, reflective, and shaped like arrowheads, some of the ships looked as though they could cut through space like a fish through water. Some of them, awkward, rusty, and cumbersome—like *The Bandolin*—seemed like they'd been docked for an eternity and it would take a gargantuan effort to get them going again. Although, all of the posted signs made it clear: miss a docking payment more than once, and your ship either left or it got toppled into the water. They'd either paid a fortune to keep them docked for an age, or the apparent write-offs still had some life left in their decrepit husks.

The sounds of the waves continuously lapped against the spaceport. Surrounded by water, whenever Seb's focus drifted, he expected the ground beneath him to sway with the tide, and a small lurch leapt through his stomach in anticipation of it.

Despite the perceived hostility from the beings in the docking bays, the more Seb looked at them, the more he noticed that not every creature looked like they wanted to murder him. The pit had been packed yesterday, so some of them must have seen what Seb could do when backed into a corner. Regardless of the blasters in their hands, some of the guards seemed slightly more hesitant about a confrontation with him.

Seb stopped outside one docking bay. Two creatures stared at him. Both were brown and had a frill of a fin that ran from between their eyes, all the way over their heads, and down their backs. With their webbed hands and feet, they looked better equipped for the sea than out in space. At first, he only heard the sound of their argument, but as he stepped closer, he made out their words.

"You let her do *what*?"

"I didn't *let* her do anything. She came over and talked to me, and the next thing I knew, she'd taken everything."

"*Everything?*"

"Not our cargo, but all of our personal belongings."

"And you did this all in the hope of getting a piece of tail?"

"Urgh," the one on the defensive said. A shake of his head and he added, "I didn't want a piece of *her* tail; she looked like a *human*. A horrible little thing, she had purple eyes and wore broken glasses."

Each docking bay had a garage-type area with a cover over the top of it. When Seb stepped into this one, it blocked off the fierce breeze and his shoulders instantly relaxed from having been clamped up to his ears.

The two guards stopped talking to one another and stared at him.

"Oh," Seb said. "Um, I—"

"What do you want?" one of the creatures said—the one who'd been angry with his mate for letting Sparks rob them.

"I couldn't help but hear you two talking about a girl." With a hand held just above his hip, Seb said, "She was about this tall, right? Glasses, purple eyes, her hair cut so sharp it could slice through steel."

"Yes," the other one said before its mate jabbed it in the ribs, clearly annoyed that it had answered.

The more aggressive of the two then looked back at Seb. "And what of it?"

Seb stepped forward and the aggressive creature raised its blaster. "I think you've come quite close enough."

Before Seb could reply, recognition dawned on the face of the other one and he pulled on his mate's arm. "You know who that is, right?"

With its blaster still raised, the aggressive one of the two shrugged. "No."

"The fighting pits. Yesterday."

The tension that had gripped the creature's amphibious features slid away and it lowered its blaster. As it re-holstered it, it said, "I'm sorry; I didn't recognise you." With its attention now on the floor, it said, "Sorry. How can we help?"

A sharp nod and Seb stepped forward again. His closeness clearly made both creatures uncomfortable, and the less aggressive one glanced over its shoulder into their cargo hold as if nervous to reveal what they carried on their ship. But they kept their weapons lowered. "Where did she go?"

"If we knew that"—the creature pointed at a steel bar that ran over Seb's head—"she'd be hanging from there."

Seb looked at the other creature, the one who'd seen Sparks. "I don't suppose you saw any jewellery on her, did you?"

"Jewellery?"

"A silver necklace—"

"That looked like a snake?"

"Yes."

"Yeah, she had it on. Nice piece."

"It's mine."

The creature visibly shrank. "Oh."

"I want it back from her. So any information you have on where I can find her would be great."

The vacant creature somehow turned more vacant in front of Seb. Its jaw fell loose, its eyes glazed, and its tongue lolled from its mouth. If the thing had started to drool at that moment, Seb would have assumed he'd slipped into a coma. "Okay, I'm guessing you know nothing, then?" Seb said. "Well, if you find her and you get a chance to get my necklace back, I'd appreciate it."

"And the girl?" the more assertive of the two asked.

"Do what you want with her. I just want my necklace back."

Both creatures nodded, and when Seb backed off, they seemed to relax a little. Who knew what the different ships carried? In Aloo, you didn't ask questions like that.

Once Seb had stepped back out onto the walkway, the wind crashed into him like it had before. It rocked him on his heels, and he pulled his coat tight again. With his scowl fixed against the wind, Seb looked at his surroundings. Wherever Sparks had got to, he'd find her.

When Seb rounded the next bend, he saw the back end of it as it ducked into one of the cargo bays. One of the tall lizard-like creatures that followed Moses everywhere, it had clearly been following Seb. Even now, as it hid in the shadows, Seb saw that it had its attention on him. Seb stared straight at it for a few seconds before he shook his head and walked off.

The sooner he left Aloo, the better.

Chapter Twenty-One

Now Seb had seen the lizard-like creature—and the lizard-like creature had seen that Seb had seen it—it abandoned its stealthy pursuit of him and followed about twenty metres behind as he strode down the walkway in between the docked ships. It no doubt had to report everything to Moses. They needed leverage to get Seb back into the pit, and the lizard had clearly been tasked with finding that leverage.

Just a few minutes after he'd left the cargo area, Seb's eyes watered again from the salty wind, and new stings ran across his bottom lip as it dried out and cracked. Too long on this planet and he'd be human jerky.

The bar Seb had visited the first night he'd arrived in Aloo sat at the end of the walkway. A handwritten sign on the outside read 'open'. The one that would have been lit up still didn't work. When Sparks blew something up, it stayed blown up. Quite impressive if she weren't such a deceptive little troll.

A crowd of creatures gathered at the side of the bar; it was a huge mass unlike any Seb had seen in Aloo, other than in the fighting pit. He walked over to check it out. It seemed that

Sparks left a trail of chaos behind her, so maybe she'd done something again.

As Seb closed in on the crowd, a few creatures turned to look at him. Before long, the entire pack had turned his way.

No doubt many of them had seen his fight because as he stepped closer, they all parted for him.

Driven by his curiosity, Seb walked around the side of the bar to the back. He found a small patch of fenced-off land. It had an archway at the front of it that read 'RESERVED FOR THE FIGHTERS IN THE PIT'. Moses must have owned the useless plot of land and turned it into a graveyard in a half-hearted gesture to ease his conscience at profiting from the deaths of hundreds. Covered in weeds and tough grass, the scratchy plot clearly couldn't be used for anything else.

The thick metal fence that surrounded the graveyard had been painted black and had large spikes along the top. When the last of the crowd parted, Seb suddenly understood the commotion and he lost his breath. "What the …?"

One of the crowd—a small green being with wings that beat so fast they turned into a blur—flew up to Seb and nodded in the direction of Mathusa. "She jumped from the roof of the bar. They found a note she'd written in her accommodation to say she should have died. She should have been given a warrior's death, but because she didn't get that, she'd have to end her life herself."

Bent over the top of the fence, the thick black spikes had been driven through Mathusa's lower back and punched up through her stomach. The dark spears glistened in the Aloo sunshine. With her legs hanging down on one side of the fence and her head hanging down on the other, she lay broken over the top of it. Blood pooled on the ground beneath her and her eyes had rolled back in her head. Her mouth hanging wide open and her skin looking paler than ever, she'd clearly been dead a while.

With the attention of the gathered mass on him, all of them clearly awaiting a reaction, Seb sighed, spun on his heel, and walked back through the crowd.

Seb marched through the bodies with his head bowed and knocked into several large creatures on the way. He passed the lizard that had been following him and glowered at it.

It spoke quietly enough so only Seb could hear. A hiss rode its words. "Now she'sss gone, Mossses will want you even more."

Seb kept his head raised and walked as if the creature hadn't said anything to him.

Chapter Twenty-Two

With the words of the lizard creature still in his mind, Seb walked away from the graveyard and the dead Mathusa. The lizard hadn't said it, but it seemed clear that they blamed Seb for Mathusa's death. He'd won the fight, nothing else. He hadn't told the crazy fool to kill herself.

Back out in the open again, Seb screwed his face up against the elements and did his best not to scratch the sore spots that grew larger with every passing moment. To touch them would be to break the scabs and invite in a rush of stinging wind. The salt stung ten times worse than the electric buzz he currently had to endure.

Away from the docking bays, Seb circumnavigated the area completely and walked along next to the ocean. The wind barrelled into him, damn near deafening him, and rocked him as he moved. Despite the lack of windbreaks, a different way back to his hotel would give him a better chance to find Sparks. She had to be somewhere. Not even someone as devious as her could get off Aloo that quickly, especially as she seemed incapable of making friends.

The bright sun reflected off the rolling ocean, and the heavy wind threw stinging droplets of salt water at Seb every time a wave broke against the spaceport. As he squinted to see better, Seb looked around for signs of Sparks. An occasional glance behind and he saw that nothing followed him. The lizards must have given up on their pursuit of him for now. They'd said their bit; maybe they thought that would be enough.

When Seb rounded the corner, his heart raced at the sight of the fighting pit. Having not come at it from this side, he stared at the back of it. When he got close enough, the huge cylindrical structure provided enough shade for him to relax the squint on his face, but just being in its presence sent a jagged anxiety rattling through his chest. This place had given him some hope of getting off the planet, but it had also clamped a ball and chain to his ankle.

No sound came from the huge pit. Too early in the day for a fight, it stood as an abandoned structure. Besides, most of the crowd probably gathered around Mathusa's broken form at that moment. Despite his enjoyment of the sport, Seb had no desire to fight again. It wouldn't be 'just one more fight'; Moses had plans for him, and Seb wanted no part of it. If he stepped back into the pit, he'd become the house fighter. Once that happened, there would be just one way out of it. He didn't plan on being found over a fence with a spike through his gut. For all Mathusa's bravado, the warrior had become Moses' slave. Whether she killed herself or not, Seb wouldn't go down that route.

When Seb walked around the front of the pit, he saw the same two guards who'd been on the door the night of his fight. The orange porcine thug seemed to instantly slip back into its hostility towards Seb and gripped its blaster as it scowled at him. It had been funny before Moses had reached out to Seb. Now he saw the guard as another one of the army of people Moses directed—one more brute who could force Seb into a situation he wanted no part of.

But it didn't matter. It didn't matter what they thought or how they tried to intimidate Seb. Whatever move Moses made, Seb would resist. With the burn of the guards' stares pressing into the side of his face, Seb looked ahead and walked straight past them. He stepped away from the pit's cover, back into the fierce wind and glaring sunshine. The harsh gales launched their flapping assault against his ears all over again.

***

Having put the pit and the hostile guards behind him, Seb passed a row of restaurants that he hadn't seen before now. All of them looked like run-down dives. Jagged shopfronts with little care given to both cleanliness and aesthetics, they clearly served as a bare essential and nothing more. None of the business owners in Aloo seemed to put much stock in appearance. In such a hostile environment, any pride in presentation would no doubt be corroded away by the elements, or the patrons, within days.

As Seb walked, he looked at all of the businesses and stopped outside a noodle bar. As ugly and run-down as the others, its windows caked in salt, paint blistered and flaking away from the woodwork, the bar still stood out as different. Something about it just …

"The lights," Seb said to himself. The only restaurant in the row to have its lights out. Sparks had been there.

As Seb approached the place, he drew a deep breath that tasted of salt. Sparks didn't leave people in a charitable mood or particularly willing to talk about how she'd screwed them over, but Seb had to find his necklace.

When he walked through the gloomy entranceway into the dark restaurant, Seb screwed his nose up at the reek of dust. An all-wooden interior—from the walls to the floor to the tables—the place looked like it had never been cleaned.

A creature rested on the bar with its back to Seb. Wiry and long-limbed, the furry, brown, bipedal being hunched over and shook its head as it muttered to itself. So quiet, Seb couldn't make out what the creature said.

When he cleared his throat, the creature spun around and glared at him. "Um," Seb said, "I've been robbed recently."

With a mouth that stretched so far around its face the edges of it almost touched its tiny ears, the corners of it turned down as the creature frowned at Seb. Its bright blue eyes fixed on him as they glowed in the darkness like fireflies. The creature shrugged its slim shoulders. "So?"

As the thing stood up to its full height of around eight feet, Seb took in its sinewy form. Long limbs, it looked like it had been made from tough old rope.

"Well, I think she's been here. She's a short, human-looking creature with purple eyes and glasses."

The blue stare of the proprietor widened as it fixed on Seb. The creature brought its clenched fist down against the bar with a loud *boom.* "You know her? How do you know she's been here?" The creature leapt over the bar and strode toward Seb. At well over eight feet tall, the being brought a wall of shadow with it and grabbed the front of Seb's shirt. A sharp yank and it pulled Seb toward it.

The stench of curdled milk came forward with the creature as it leaned close. So rancid, Seb pulled back and tried to breathe through his mouth.

Seb's world threatened to turn into slow motion as the creature leaned in and the heat of its stale breath pushed against Seb's face. "*How* do you know she's been here?"

"The lights," Seb said.

"Huh?"

"That's her thing. She upsets someone and then blows their electricity. Like an extra kick in the gut, you know. She's a spiteful little rat."

The restaurant owner released its grip on Seb and stepped back a pace. After a heavy sigh, its slim shoulders slumped and it looked at the ground. "She came here last night, ordered the biggest order we've had in years, ate the lot, and then asked for credit. When it became clear she couldn't pay, we locked her out back. We had a few other clients in, so we planned on dealing with her after they'd gone. Except … she escaped. The first we knew of it was when the power went out. We went out back to find she'd busted free. Not only did she blow the lights, but every electrical appliance in the place too." A shake ran through the creature's voice as it clearly struggled to control its rage. "All of our food's going to go off. She's put us out of business."

The creature clearly didn't know her whereabouts. Like many of the other beings that wanted Sparks—Seb included—if they got their hands on the little snake, they would have snapped her neck by now. After a heavy sigh, Seb nodded. "Thank you. If I find her, I'll make sure I bring her back here so she can be held accountable for her actions."

Clearly defeated, the long creature stood with its arms hanging down and its head dropped. "Thank you."

Without another word, Seb left the restaurant.

***

Seb returned to the hotel, none the wiser on Sparks' whereabouts. Although, she probably still remained on Aloo. The restaurant owner had seen her the previous night, so she had to be somewhere.

Sore from the salty wind and exhausted from his day, he walked across the hotel's foyer to get to his room. Before he could make it to the stairs that led up to the floor he stayed on, the receptionist called to him.

With a heavy sigh, Seb walked over to her. "Is it urgent?" he said. "I've had a long day and I could really do with resting up."

The receptionist looked down at the desk in front of her. "Um ... well ... it's just ... it's ... um." Her two heads spoke in turn.

A rush of anger snapped through Seb, and he spoke through a clenched jaw. "Just say it."

"Your rent has gone up."

"Huh?"

"To fifteen hundred credits per night."

A deep breath and Seb glared at the receptionist as his world slipped into slow motion.

"Moses forced us to do it."

Seb bit down so hard on his jaw it ran pains up each side of his face. As much as he wanted to shout at the receptionist, it wouldn't do any good. His world sped up again. "Okay, I'll pack my things and leave, then."

"Um ..."

"What?" Seb shouted, his voice echoing through the hotel's abandoned and cavernous foyer.

"We're the only place on Aloo that's allowed to have you as a guest. Every other place has been instructed to turn you away."

With his heart beating hard enough to burst from his chest, Seb turned away from the receptionist. She didn't deserve to be on the end of his fury. Moses had made the call, not her. Without another word, Seb walked back to his room and his feet dragged as he went. He'd have to get off Aloo sooner rather than later. If he hadn't found Sparks within a day, he'd get out of there. With enough credits left on his card, he could afford one night in the hotel at their new price, and hopefully a safe passage off the damn planet with the change.

Chapter Twenty-Three

Before that night, if Seb had imagined staying in a hotel worth fifteen hundred credits, he would have imagined luxury beyond compare. A bed so soft that when he lay on it, he sank to the point where it felt like the mattress gave him a warm hug. Room service with anything and everything he could imagine, and all of it included in the bill. Hell, he'd even get woken with a massage every morning. As it was, Seb had the worst night's sleep of his entire life. The mattress had so many lumps he might as well have slept on a sack of rocks. The wind's cold fingers found their way through the smallest gaps into his room and poked and prodded him all night. The light from the hallway outside slipped through the large gap beneath the door to the point where he might as well have had the light on in his room, and the wafer-thin duvet felt like sleeping beneath old newspaper. At one hundred credits per night, none of it mattered, but his perception of what he found acceptable had been drastically altered by the hike in price.

Up with the crack of dawn, Seb packed his small bag. Even a small bag had room to spare because he had so few belongings—and they numbered even less since Sparks had robbed him. He had enough credits to pay for last night's stay and, with any luck, enough left to buy a safe passage away from Aloo.

After he'd shouldered his backpack, he scanned his grimy room and shook his head. "Fifteen hundred credits per night. Ridiculous."

***

Down in the hotel's reception, Seb smiled at the receptionist and handed his key to her. Now he'd had several interactions with her, he'd learned to look from one of her eyes to the other, not lingering on either one for too long.

"You're leaving?" she asked.

"You expect me to stay with the rates you're charging?"

"Well, it seems that Moses wants something. I assumed Moses would get what he wanted and we could go back to charging you a sensible rate for the room."

Seb scoffed. "Not a chance. That criminal won't bully me into fighting in the pit. No way."

Before the receptionist could say anything else, Seb nodded at her. "Thank you anyway. I understand that you could only charge me what Moses told you to charge me. I'm starting to see the power he has in this place, which is another reason for me to move on. Moses doesn't seem like the kind of man to do business with."

The receptionist looked over into the corner of the foyer with both of her heads. Because the creature had been in the shadows, Seb hadn't noticed him. Now he'd seen him, he seemed so damn obviously there. Seb stared at the lizard creature that had followed him the day before. With its clawed and three-fingered hand resting on its blaster, it scowled back at Seb.

After a heavy sigh, Seb turned back to the receptionist. "See, Moses clearly isn't a man to get involved with. The sooner I get away from this place, the better."

Paler than she'd been at the start of their conversation, the receptionist nodded before she picked up Seb's room key, turned her back on him, and filed it away.

Seb walked across the foyer and watched the lizard creature, who watched him straight back. His footsteps echoed in the quiet and cavernous space, and the hinges on the front door creaked when Seb pushed it open and walked outside into Aloo's bitter wind.

***

The change from the dark hotel foyer to the bright sun stung Seb's eyes and he made a visor with his hand. The harsh wind burned the sores that had formed on his face. No other beings seemed to suffer with the atmosphere. Human skin didn't have much resistance to Aloo's weather.

By the time Seb had walked a little way from the hotel, the lizard creature stepped out of the building to follow him. Hardly a surprise, really. Although what could it do? It had no reason to take any kind of action, and Seb had evidently said no to Moses. No way could the gangster force him to do anything he didn't want to.

Before he could pick the holes in his own rationale, Seb looked across the spaceport and froze. About twenty metres from where he stood, hovering around the mouth of an alley, he saw Sparks.

Without thinking, Seb pointed at the girl and screamed, "You!"

Every creature between Seb and Sparks turned to look at him—although he didn't care. Seb broke into a sprint. With the wind in his face, his eyes watering from the salty onslaught, he remained focused on the small woman and ran with all he had.

Before he got to her, Sparks ducked down the alley she'd hovered in front of. But she wouldn't get away. Not now. No way.

The second Seb entered the alley after her, an explosion of light blew up in front of him. A vast magnesium flare, it dazzled and temporarily blinded him, forcing him to stagger backwards. Seb stopped and rubbed his eyes, but no matter how vigorous his action, he couldn't coax his vision back.

With his heart on overdrive, Seb stood still, vulnerable to an attack from anywhere. No doubt the lizard remained on his tail. "Sparks!" he screamed, so loud it tore at his throat. "Where the hell are you?"

A few seconds later his world came slowly back into view. The shop that she'd rigged to blow seemed like some kind of convenience store. What must have been the owner—a slug-like creature with a Mohawk—had come out the front and scratched its head as it stared at the destruction.

When Seb checked behind, the lizard creature seemed to have gone. However, that didn't mean anything; it could be anywhere. Seb would be an idiot to think he wasn't being watched for the entire time he stayed on Aloo. He walked up the alley toward the shop owner. At least if he told the creature that his power wouldn't be back on for some time, it would allow it to maybe save some of the stock that would otherwise go off in the broken fridges and freezers.

But when Seb got to the shop at the end of the alley, the tight space opened up into a huge square and he saw her again. Across the other side, she was just about to round a bend behind a restaurant. With most of his vision back, Seb took off after the little rat again.

***

Puffed out from the run, Seb kept on Sparks' tail as he came to the side of the restaurant and saw her disappear around another bend. She might be cunning, but with small legs, she wouldn't outrun him.

When he rounded the next corner, Seb watched the little girl lift a metal cover from the road and disappear down into Aloo's sewers. No wonder she remained hidden if she lived down there. The streets above were a vile place to exist, so the sewers had to be positively revolting. With one final chance to get his dad's necklace back before he left Aloo, Seb followed after her.

Seb climbed down the ladder into the sewers. Just two rungs down the heady reek of the waste of a thousand different creatures hit him like an uppercut. He had to hold on tight to the metal ladder to prevent himself from falling into the gaseous stink. Yet he pushed on, down into the dingy underworld of Aloo.

Although a river of sludge flowed beneath the city, an elevated footpath ran alongside it. Seb would have waded through the mess if it meant getting his dad's necklace back. Thankfully, the high ceiling and walkway meant he didn't have to.

Although he'd lost sight of Sparks now, mainly because of just how dark it had gotten beneath Aloo's streets, he heard footsteps and followed after them.

The sewers ran like train tunnels beneath the city. Every few hundred metres, a bridge would cross over and link one footpath to the other.

Dark, although not completely pitch black, Seb followed the sound of the retreating Sparks, which fortunately led him toward the light.

With just a few metres to go, Seb noticed the light he homed in on flickered. It had seemed like a natural illumination, but now he'd gotten closer to it, he recognised it as the beam of a torch. But why would they light this place with torches? Maybe more than Sparks lived down here. Although, on a planet where anything went because of their lack of law enforcement, it seemed odd that beings would choose to come down here voluntarily. No matter; Seb hadn't come for a visit. He would get to Sparks, get the necklace, and get out.

When Seb got to the end of the tunnel, he poked his head around the corner and froze. The Sparks that he'd been chasing stood in full view in the centre of a wide-open space where several tunnels converged. As he stared at her, his heart sank and he whispered, "A hologram."

When the hologram flickered and vanished, Seb looked up at the other creatures gathered there, and they looked back at him. A quick head count showed eight of them. Two of them were the creatures he'd seen the other day, the ones with the fins that ran from between their eyes, over their heads, and down their backs—the ones that Sparks had robbed. At the time, the slippery creatures acted like they'd had something to hide, but Seb ignored it. Everyone in Aloo acted like they had something to hide. As he looked at the six others, all of them brutes, all of them a different species, and all of them packing at least one blaster each, his entire being sank. Sparks had well and truly set him up. She knew that these creatures wouldn't let anyone set eyes on the deal and walk away afterwards.

The eight crooks stood around two large crates, both with three creatures in each. Seb had just busted a slave trade. When he looked at the young captives, clearly all children, he ground his jaw.

Something in their eyes pulled on Seb's heart. Sure, captured children would always upset him, but he saw something of himself in them. Children without their parents. That couldn't happen.

From the look on the faces of those doing the deal, they didn't plan on letting Seb leave. But Seb had plans of his own.

Chapter Twenty-Four

Seb stepped out into the open space in full view of the creatures and nodded in the direction of the cages. They'd seen him, so there seemed little point in being anything other than direct. With a clenched jaw, he feigned politeness. "Sorry to break up your trade, but I can't let this happen."

As one, all eight of the creatures outside the cages raised their blasters and pointed them at Seb. Everything slipped into slow motion at that point. The elongated words of the creatures facing him rose in volume and dragged out as deep and indecipherable calls. With so many enemies around, the weak spots of each flashed through Seb's mind, and he struggled to focus on which one to attack first.

The pavements that ran alongside the river of waste were wider in the intersection, so Seb had room to dart to the side as the first stream of blaster fire came at him.

The blasts moved in slow motion like everything else, but the sheer volume of them meant he avoided all but one. As he dodged to the side, a searing hot pain ran across his left ear and he caught the smell of his own cauterised flesh. Rich and sickly sweet, his ear screamed with the pain of it.

For the briefest second, everything sped up, but Seb found his flow again and pulled his world back under control.

While moving forward, Seb dodged and rolled to avoid another hit from one of the blasters. They'd tear through his flesh with ease, so he kept his wits and bobbed and weaved, making progress toward the slavers the entire time.

When he got to the creature at the front of the pack—a wiry thing no taller than him and probably half his weight—Seb grabbed its arm and forced its elbow the wrong way with a deep *crack.*

The creature screamed and dropped its blaster. With everything moving so slowly, Seb had time to catch the weapon as it fell and drove a punch across the creature's chin. By the time the creature hit the ground, it had gone limp from the blow. Leaving it sprawled out on the cold concrete path, Seb jumped aside as another wave of blaster fire came his way.

Because of the slow motion, Seb saw it before it happened and winced. Several of the blasts, aimed at where he had been, hit the being he'd just knocked down and ran straight through it. Although initially unconscious from Seb's knockout punch, the criminal wouldn't ever wake up again.

With his stolen blaster raised, Seb returned fire. Although he might have done many things, he didn't kill when he didn't have to. He fired six shots in quick succession and scored four hits, each of them a leg wound to a different creature. As they fell one by one, Seb moved forward, always closing down the space between them and him.

Another shot exploded the kneecap of a large monster on the

other side of the brown river. With a loud scream, it reached for the wound and toppled forward into the sludge below.

A heave rose in Seb's throat as he listened to the muddy squelch from where the beast landed in the waste.

The only two creatures that remained standing were the ones Seb had met outside their ship. Identical to his untrained eye, they stood side by side, their brown Mohawk fins wobbling as they shook their heads. The two amphibious creatures only lasted longer than the others because the cowards had made their way to the back of the pack. Seb ran at them.

Two quick leg sweeps and he dropped the pair of them. With his attention on their noses, Seb whacked each one. Their eyes rolled back in their heads.

One by one, Seb sparked each of the four remaining smugglers. So consumed with the agony of having their legs shot, they didn't even look up as Seb moved down the line and delivered a knockout blow to each one in turn. Three of them needed a whack to the head, but one required a sharp chop to the neck to turn its lights out.

The world around Seb returned to normal speed. Six unconscious bodies surrounded him. One more lay dead, and the other one had gone the way of the river of waste. Sure, it could come back and attack him, but it would have to overcome the raging torrent of excrement with a blown-out knee first.

Seb walked over to the cages. The tiny creatures inside all shook as they held onto the bars and stared through them with wide eyes. One of the finned creatures had dropped a key when it fell; Seb picked it up and opened both cages.

At first, the children pulled away from Seb and huddled at

the back of their prisons. To watch them hurt his heart. It didn't bear thinking about what had happened to the poor things to get them to this point. The least he could do was make sure they got back to their parents.

Seb hunched down and held his hand out toward them. "You can come out now. You're free."

The children still didn't move.

"I promise you, I won't hurt you."

Still, the children said nothing and remained where they were.

"Where are your parents?"

One of the children, a small grey creature with a horn in the centre of its face, spoke up. "They're up above. We were taken yesterday from them." With wide eyes, it looked over at the traffickers. "I heard them say they would get us off Aloo before our parents found us."

"Okay," Seb said, "so you know where to find them?"

All of the children nodded this time.

"If I deal with the bad creatures down here, can you find your way back?" Seb pointed to the tunnel he'd emerged from. "Just go that way and you'll come to a ladder that leads to the surface. I'll be following behind shortly, so I'll make sure you made it out, okay?"

The children came out of their cages one by one. None of them stood any taller than about two feet. A bridge ran over the river of sludge, which Seb pointed at. "Cross there, and then run as fast as you can."

When wide eyes and pursed lips stared up at him, Seb added, "Or you could wait for me and I'll show you the way out."

What looked like the oldest of the group shook its head. "No, thank you. We've been down here too long. We'll find our way out." With a trembling hand, it reached out to Seb and squeezed the top of his arm. "Thank you for saving us."

As the children walked away, Seb looked at the downed beings. He then faced the damp ceiling above him. "I'm sure you understand, Dad. As an officer of the law, you would have done the same thing." Impossible not to smile, Seb added, "Although, probably not as well as I just did it."

Before he could answer himself in his dad's condemning voice, Seb walked over to the first of the fishy creatures, rifled through its pockets, and took everything out. He then dragged it over to the open cage and wedged it inside.

***

By the time he'd put the last of the traffickers into the cages and locked both doors, Seb had to stop and wipe the perspiration from his brow. His left ear throbbed from where he'd been shot, and sweat ran into the wound.

With a pile of belongings on the ground outside the cages, Seb sat down and rifled through them.

One of the creatures came to while he did it. "Hey, what are you doing?"

As Seb watched the horrible being squirm and twist in its cramped space, he smiled. "I'm deciding what's worth taking and what I should throw in the sludge."

"Do you know who I am?"

"I don't care who you are. I'm taking what I want from here. And you know what? Most beings won't care who you are either.

Once you've rotted in that cage with the rest of your nasty pals, you'll be no more than a memory. And you probably won't even be that."

The cage rattled as the creature grabbed the barred door and shook it. The noise roused some of the others. Before long, all of them had come to and focused their fury on Seb.

After he'd cleaned out anything worth taking, Seb stood up and used his foot to sweep the rest of their belongings into the river of crap. Despite their value on the black market—the only market Aloo had—Seb dropped the blasters in too. This generated the most vehement protests from the slavers in the cages.

"Do you know how much a blaster costs?"

"You're paying me back for that, you know."

"Why would you throw them away?"

Yet none of their complaints provoked much in Seb; he turned his back on the creatures and walked away in the direction of the bridge the children had crossed.

Halfway across, Seb held up the key that unlocked the cage for all of the creatures to see. "I'll tell you what. To make it fair, I'm going to leave this key here." He bent down and placed it on the bridge. "You seem like a resourceful bunch, so I'm sure you'll work out how to get to it and free yourselves."

The creatures in the cage had finally gone quiet, but each of them levelled their own brand of rage at Seb.

With a broad smile, Seb stood back up again and said, "You know what? You lot don't deserve a chance. What would have been the chances for those poor bastards that you were about to ship off to who knows where?" With his toe touching the key on the walkway, Seb shifted his foot forward and knocked the key off the side into the sludge below. It landed with the gentlest *plop*, sat on top of the body of acrid gloop for a few seconds, and then disappeared into the thick goo as it churned with its movement.

After a quick salute to the traffickers, Seb jogged back the way he'd come. The angry threats from those in the cages chased after him.

Just before he rounded the bend out of sight, he looked over at the raging faces and threw them the bird. When he turned back around, a bright white light exploded across his vision. The punch turned his legs bandy, and as he fell to the ground, Seb's world turned dark.

Chapter Twenty-Five

The pain in the back of Seb's eyes when he opened them streaked through his eyeballs like inch-long metal splinters. The boom of a deep headache pulsed through his face and crushed his skull. The air around him stank of halitosis. The stench hung so heavy, it lay against his dry tongue as a funk that tasted like he'd licked old trainers. Smothered in complete darkness, it didn't matter how many times he blinked, his vision wouldn't clear.

As Seb woke up more, he became aware of the rough fabric of the sack over his head that rubbed against his skin, clawing at the sores around his eyes, nose, and mouth. Heavy and coarse, it lay against his face, and with his hands cuffed behind his back, he could do nothing to lift it away.

With a numb arse from the cold metal floor, Seb leaned against a wall equally as frigid. The very slight hum of a spaceship vibrated through the structure. It felt like they were travelling at high speed, but he couldn't be sure.

Despite the dryness that stretched through Seb's throat, permeating every part of it and making it hard to speak, he said, "Hello?"

At first, no one responded.

"Hello?"

Still nothing.

Just before he said it a third time, a meek female voice replied, "Hello."

Seb's heart raced and he shifted closer to the voice to hear her better. He spoke quickly. "Where am I?"

"I … I don't know. I can't see anything. I was hoping you'd be able to tell me."

"I can't see anything either. You have a sack over your head too?"

"And my hands are tied."

No matter how many times Seb blinked, he couldn't get rid of his headache. With his head tilted forward, he looked at the floor to let the sack hang away from his face. It did little for the reek, but eased the pressure of the heavy fabric and took the sting from his sores. "Where have you come from?"

"Aloo."

"Me too. Someone jumped me and I woke up here. Is that what happened to you?"

The female said, "Yep."

"Damn. I'm Seb, by the way."

The girl went quiet.

"Hello? Did you hear me? I'm Seb."

"I heard you, Seb."

The haze that Seb had existed in because of the knockout blow suddenly lifted. How'd he not heard it before now? "Sparks?"

The girl went quiet.

"Is that you?" As Seb fought to hold the fury from his voice, he tried again, "Well, is it?"

"I'm sorry, Seb, I shouldn't have robbed you."

"You little rat." Seb kicked in the direction of the girl. Instead of connecting with the villainous little snake, his shin caught something metal and a wave of hot nauseating pain rushed up his leg. With his teeth clenched, Seb screamed so loud it hurt, "Ow!"

The sound of Sparks' voice got farther away as she clearly backed away from him. "I said I'm sorry."

"Well, that's all right then. You only robbed me blind, which forced me into the fighting pit and led me into this hot mess. I have no doubt that I'm here now because I fought publicly. I don't know where I'm going or what's planned for me, but I do know that if I hadn't met you, I'd be getting by and working out a way to leave Aloo."

"At least that part of the plan came off," Sparks said. "Although I'm not sure we're going somewhere better than Aloo."

Even though she'd moved farther away, Seb still kicked in Sparks' direction. This time, he caught nothing but fresh air. "You're a damn parasite. Where are my things?"

Sparks didn't reply.

"I said where are my things?"

"I'm not going to talk to you while you're shouting. If you speak to me nicely, then maybe we can have a conversation."

"Talk to you nicely? What the hell? You robbed me, you little snake. You're lucky I don't come over there and wring your skinny little neck."

"With cuffed hands?"

"No one likes a smart-ass, Sparks. Or a thief for that matter. You were out of line robbing me like you did, especially after I bought you those drinks. I swear if it's the last thing I do, I'll break you after I get my things back from you."

"Look, Sebastian—"

"No one calls me that."

"All right, Sebastian."

Seb's rage raised his body temperature to the point where his face sweated beneath the sack. As he sat there, he took deep breaths to prevent his world from slipping into slow motion. His talent would serve no purpose at that moment.

"Anyway," Sparks continued, "as I was saying, I think we have more to worry about than an old piece of tin."

"It wasn't tin."

"It was; I had it tested."

Silence.

"Anyway, like I was saying, we have more to worry about than a necklace and some credits. Where are we? Where are we headed?"

Nothing else mattered to Seb at that moment but revenge. Without another word, he shuffled close to Sparks as quietly as he could.

"Sebastian? Are you still there?"

Seb used her voice to guide him. When he felt like he'd gotten to within a metre or two, he yelled and launched himself in her direction like a fish leaping from water. Another bright light flashed, and the *tonk* of his head connecting with a hard wall echoed through his skull. Seb's entire world rocked and he fell flat.

As he lay on the floor, the sharp pain returned to his eyeballs. Seb clenched his jaw and spoke through gritted teeth. "You little—"

Then everything else faded away as he passed out again.

Chapter Twenty-Six

Seb woke from his second knockout blow. His hands were now free of the cuffs, and the sack had been removed from his head. Although his headache endured, it had diminished somewhat and had shifted so it throbbed through his sinuses rather than his eyeballs. The sores around his eyes, nose, mouth, and even the burn on his ear buzzed. When he grabbed his forehead and felt the lump from headbutting whatever it was he'd headbutted, he winced at the sharp sting.

Seb sat up and squinted against the bright light. The sores at the edges of his eyes stung from the involuntary action. When Seb put his feet down, the cold floor burned his bare soles. The short and sharp shock dragged him into the present moment. Before he could think about the disappearance of his shoes, he suddenly realised what his surroundings looked like. With an exhausted groan, he looked around his tiny cell. "What the …?"

On the bottom bunk of two beds, Seb looked at the steel door that locked them in. It had a small window criss-crossed with bars. To one side sat a toilet without a seat or toilet paper.

If he stood up, he'd be able to walk six paces from wall to wall and no more.

When Seb tried to look up, what felt like a trapped nerve ran a blinding shock of electric pain down his neck and spine. Instead, he banged his fist against the underside of the bunk above him.

A second later, the deep male voice of his cellmate called down, "What?"

"Where am I?"

"*The Black Hole.*"

"Huh?"

"*The Black Hole.*"

The bed, although steel, groaned and shifted above Seb as his cellmate moved around. When he jumped down, the floor shook from the impact. "I wondered how long it would take you to come round."

A Mandulu, the big dumb creature stood in front of Seb and stared at him with half a smile on its stupid face. It had the same broken horns common with its species that protruded from its bottom jaw and up over its top lip. Just looking at the thing made Seb want to hit it. Whenever he came into contact with the idiot race, it always ended in a fight.

For as much as Seb stared at the Mandulu, the Mandulu stared back at Seb. It breathed through its nose with deep puffs that rocked its huge frame. Large shoulders and massive biceps, the creature balled its fists and tilted its fat head to one side. "You got a problem, pal?"

And he did have a problem. But 'Yeah, I can't stand your entire species' didn't seem to fit, so Seb didn't voice it. Instead, he said, "So how do you know what this place is called?"

"You've not heard of *The Black Hole* before?"

"Should I have?"

The Mandulu laughed a deep laugh. "It's only the largest prison ship in the galaxy. You're on a floating behemoth that—because it never docks—answers to no one. You have no rights on this ship. You must have done something pretty bad to end up here."

"What did *you* do?"

The Mandulu's red eyes narrowed as he looked at Seb.

"So where was I before they brought me here?" Seb said.

"I'm guessing they had you in a holding bay."

"And the girl I was with?"

The Mandulu's face dropped. "How would I know? I've been in here the entire time."

A cold chill snapped through Seb, so he pulled his feet beneath him and dragged his bedding around his shoulders.

"Why didn't they bring me straight here in the first place?"

"How would I know? I've been here the entire time. Although, *The Black Hole* is notorious for overcrowding, even with its processing policy, so maybe they needed to wait for a space to become free."

"Processing policy?"

"Yeah. You don't get a fair trial once you end up on this ship. You get processed in thirty days, regardless of your pleas of innocence. My last cellmate hit day thirty this morning, which is why you're now sleeping in his bed."

The way the Mandulu spoke, drip-feeding Seb information as it rode some kind of power trip, wound Seb even tighter.

Maybe he should just bang the dumb creature out and be done with it. It would save them all a lot of hassle.

When Seb didn't reply, the Mandulu clearly felt too excited about the information it had to remain quiet. "When they process you, you never return."

"So they kill you?"

"Process you. They call it processing." The dumb oaf grinned. "But I'd call it killing, yeah."

"Why are you so damn smug about it? Surely you'll be there sooner than me."

The Mandulu nodded. "Yep. But trust me; by the time you've spent more than a few hours in this cell, you'll look forward to processing too."

"Is there any way to avoid it?"

A shake of its head and the Mandulu laughed. The mirth fell from its face a second later, and it said, "No."

Chapter Twenty-Seven

After a long sleep, Seb woke to find his headache had eased somewhat. With lucidity came the acceptance that he still remained in the cold cell. When he lifted his head from his pillow, his tacky left ear pulled on the fabric from having been seared by the blaster fire in the sewers of Aloo. The cauterised wound had broken apart while he slept. Before he'd thought about it, he let the yawn out that demanded to be released. It simultaneously ripped open the sores around his nose, mouth, and eyes.

Seb sat up in bed, his face and head wrapped in the gentle buzz from the pain of his wounds, and saw the cumbersome Mandulu pacing up and down the tiny space.

"Jeez, son," the Mandulu said when he saw Seb had woken, "you were out for hours. Do you deal with all of your problems by going to sleep?" Black bags sat beneath the creature's eyes and mania rode his words. "You only have thirty days left; you should try to experience them on some level before they process you."

For a halfwit, the Mandulu had hit the truth on the head.

The bit about Seb sleeping on his problems at least. A thirty-day all-nighter didn't seem like the best use of Seb's time in the cell unless he planned on going to processing with a frazzled mind and no grip on reality. But, as his cellmate had pointed out, Seb had always had an ability to sleep. The more stressful his life got, the better he dozed. The best night's sleeps he'd ever had had come after his mum had died, his brother had gone to prison for murder, and his dad's passing. The first night in the cell came pretty close to those experiences. After he'd found out about *The Black Hole* and how they dealt with their prisoners, he shut down. The reality of his situation overwhelmed his tired mind.

"Okay, then," the Mandulu said at Seb's lack of reply.

Before Seb's cellmate could say anything else, the hatch at the bottom of their cell door snapped open with a sharp *crack*. A tray with two bowls of brown slop came through the hole, and it closed again with another *crack*.

The clumsy Mandulu bent down and lifted their food. He turned to Seb and handed him a bowl and spoon before he took his own and discarded the metal tray. It clattered against the steel floor, and the sound jangled through Seb's body as it set his nerves on edge.

For the first few seconds, Seb stared at the sludge in the bowl. It looked similar to the river in the sewers. Fighting back a heave, Seb plunged his spoon into it. But before he could lift it out again, his Mandulu cellmate stepped on his bunk to climb up to the top. The pressure of its heavy foot tilted Seb to one side, and he had to keep his bowl level as he bobbed and swayed on his thin mattress.

The bed rocked for a few seconds before the Mandulu above finally settled down. Confident he could eat again, Seb lifted the bowl to just beneath his mouth and raised a spoonful of the sludge to his lips. The meal stank. It had a muddy reek like peat, with a slight hint of grass to it. As Seb listened to the Mandulu above him slurp the horrible liquid, he shook his head and took a mouthful of the lukewarm paste.

It tasted like it smelled. Not necessarily offensive, more like he'd eaten a big slice of lawn.

Grunting and slobbering above him, the Mandulu slurped away before he finally said, "I'm here because I could never behave."

As Seb watched a drop of the Mandulu's dinner fall and land on his leg, he ground his jaw and drew deep breaths.

"I just couldn't back down from a fight, you know. I had to keep moving from planet to planet because of the trouble I caused. I'd fight in the fighting pits when I could. I'm undefeated, don't you know." After a pause to slurp his slop, the Mandulu spilled another dribble onto Seb's knee and said, "But I just had to fight. We're a fighting race. It's what we're meant to do."

"You could have said no," Seb said, like he'd mastered that skill.

With the Mandulu's deep laughter came more drops of the brown slop. The edges of Seb's world hazed slightly, and he fought to pull himself away from the slow motion.

"Yeah, right," the Mandulu said. "I'm guessing you don't know much about fighting, little man?"

A deep sigh and Seb shook his head. "No. I guess not." He tasted another mouthful of the muddy sludge.

"Well, let me tell you, when you have my fighting skills and someone challenges you, you take the challenge. You understand?"

Deep breaths and Seb remained silent.

"The people who run *The Black Hole* are bounty hunters. There was a price on my head and they came to collect it. I'd had so many planets file murder charges against me that they must have been paid well to catch me. The rats snatched me with my pants down. They lured me into a honeytrap. That was another weakness of mine: the brothels."

Again, Seb said nothing as he listened to his cellmate snort with laughter.

"So," the Mandulu said, "you must have done something serious to end up here."

"I don't know why I'm here," Seb said. "Mistaken identity probably."

"Or maybe just the fact that you're human."

"What's that supposed to mean?"

"Well, everyone hates humans, right?"

Seb rolled his eyes. "Right."

"You invade planet after planet and take control of them when they've done nothing to you. You're such a paranoid species that you start wars on other people before they can start wars on you. The conflict's in your head."

"Don't you just love pop psychology?"

"Huh?"

"Don't worry; please carry on with your enlightened assessment of my species."

The floor shook when the Mandulu leapt from his bunk and landed in front of Seb. The stench of his rancid breath came forward with the Mandulu's large chin. With his broken tusks just millimetres from Seb's face, the hideous creature roared so loud it blew Seb's hair back and smothered him in a stench worse than any toilet Seb had visited.

A shake ran through Seb as he placed his half-finished meal down on the floor. He then got to his feet, forcing the Mandulu back a step, and stood directly in front of it, staring up into its red eyes. He said nothing.

"Are you mocking me, you pitiful little human?"

Again, Seb remained quiet and simply stared into the Mandulu's ugly face.

"Because you're a fool if you are. This can only end one way."

The world around Seb blurred at the edges again as the creature before him slipped into slow motion. He didn't try to stifle it this time. Like the Mandulu he'd fought in the bar, this one's bulbous chin presented itself as the place to hit. One sharp punch and he'd spark the thing. However, something else tugged at Seb's attention. To his left, in his peripheral vision, he felt the presence of something. When he looked at the wall behind the toilet, he suddenly saw its weakness. Like the Mandulu's chin, it would take one well-aimed punch to break it.

So close to the Mandulu, Seb could see the pores on its leathered skin. A deep breath, and he swung for him. As true as ever, he hit the beast clean and watched the creature's eyes roll back before it folded to the floor. The lump crashed down so hard, the cell door rattled in its frame. Hopefully the guards wouldn't come to investigate.

Still locked in slow motion, Seb crossed the cell and threw a punch at the wall behind the toilet. The steel panel that had looked solid to Seb's normal eye bent like it had been made from foil and fell away to reveal what looked like the ship's ventilation system.

With the Mandulu out cold on the floor, Seb returned to him and kicked him so hard on the nose it hurt his ankle. It would feel that when it came to. Without a second thought, Seb returned to the hole in the wall, stood up on the metal toilet, and climbed into the darkness of the ventilation shaft.

Chapter Twenty-Eight

If there was anything in the galaxy that Seb hated more than tight tunnels and Mandulus, he'd not encountered it yet. And he'd had to tolerate them both on the same day. As he commando crawled along the ship's ventilation shaft, the sound of his own breath echoed in the enclosed space. Whatever he had to go through, it had to be better than spending any more time in that cell—it certainly had to be better than getting *processed.*

The metal ventilation shaft had been made up of thousands of square tubes. A lip rose up where each one had been joined to the next, so every ten metres or so, Seb would drag his body over another one. The first few had been no big deal, but after crossing lump after lump, the cumulative sting in his elbows and knees turned into a sharp pain that remained even when he didn't cross a join.

With the sound of the prison below and above, Seb pulled himself along, his heart in his throat. Better to die trying to escape than to accept his fate like his dumb cellmate had. No way would they process him. No way.

At an intersection, Seb looked left, right, and then straight ahead. One choice would be as good as any. With no idea where his cell sat in relation to the rest of the prison ship, he couldn't even guess what direction he should head in to escape. He continued straight and would continue to do so as long as straight presented itself as an option. If *The Black Hole* came anywhere near the Mandulu's description of it, Seb could be in the shafts indefinitely, lost as he tried to find his way out.

Every once in a while, Seb found himself over a grate. Just about wide enough for him to slip through, one of them would provide his way out. As of yet, he'd not found the one he'd be prepared to take a chance on.

***

Seb had crawled for about twenty minutes when he came to the ventilation shaft that stopped him dead. The room below seemed different to the ones he'd seen. A storage room of some description, it looked to house the confiscated belongings of all the prisoners. At least, Seb guessed it to be for all of the prisoners. The vast room had items stacked from floor to ceiling, many of them in clear plastic bags as if they were to be used as evidence in a trial on a planet that actually cared about justice. Not so many of them left.

There had to be something useful down there, but the room would no doubt be locked up tighter than most of the cells. If he got down, he might not be able to get back out again. Then he saw it.

On top of one of the crates, in its own clear plastic bag, sat Sparks' mini-computer. A quick search and Seb didn't see anything else he recognised, no wallet of his, and more importantly, no necklace. However, if he had Sparks' computer, he had a bargaining chip to get his dad's necklace back should he ever find her again.

The vent had no screws in it, so it came away with a *pop*. The blood rushed to Seb's head and made him dizzy when he leaned down to look into the room. Full of goods, but empty of people, Seb lowered himself, legs first, into the storage area.

With his entire lower body dangling down into the room, vulnerable should anyone walk in at that moment, Seb let go and dropped the last few feet.

When Seb landed, he fell to the floor and clattered into a stack of crates. For the briefest moment, he froze at the loud *crash*. For what good that would do; he couldn't take the noise back. What an idiot. When Seb heard the heavy footsteps of what must have been guards running toward the storage room, he grabbed Sparks' mini-computer and stacked some crates one on top of the other beneath the hole he'd just slipped through. There seemed no point in hiding in the room among the personal belongings. If they found him, he had nowhere to go.

A shake ran through Seb's arms as he layered one crate on top of another. He couldn't help but notice all of the confiscated items as he stacked them. Wallets, navigation devices, cigarettes ... for all of the junk he saw, he didn't see a single blaster. They must have been stored somewhere else.

The footfalls that approached the room got closer with every second.

A wobbly tower at best, Seb jumped up onto the newly stacked crates in time to hear the beeps from the security lock on the door. It sounded like a guard entering a code to access the room.

The crates swayed beneath Seb's feet as he reached up through the hole in the shaft. In his panic, he climbed up the wrong way, so he faced back down the shaft the way he'd come. Not that he planned on heading back to his cell.

As Seb pushed the last of himself up into the shaft, the crates beneath his feet toppled and fell. A loud clatter accompanied his scrabble to get away.

The second he'd pulled himself up, he heard the door swish open and the guards rush into the room. Although gassed, Seb fought to slow his breaths as he slid the grate back over the hole. It made the slightest *click* when it slotted into place.

Every part of Seb wanted to rush, from his shaking limbs to his rapid pulse, but he fought against it. It would make too much noise and blow his cover for sure. A blaster would make light work of the thin metal of the ventilation shaft should one of the guards choose to shoot. As he shifted backwards down the shaft, Seb listened to the guards walk through the storage room and heard their conversation.

"I can't see anything, can you?"

A pause and the other one replied, "Nothing, no. I'm guessing the crates just fell over again."

With a view below through the grate, Seb watched the guards. They both wore hats with their uniform, so Seb couldn't tell their species. Although, with the little travelling he'd done, he didn't recognise many species other than his own. If they didn't frequent the fighting pits, he wouldn't be familiar with them. One of the guards stood tall and wide, the other one much more slight.

"Shall we call it in?" the smaller guard said.

"Yeah, it won't do any harm."

The small guard's radio hissed when he lifted it to his mouth. "We heard a disturbance in the storage room, although we can't see anyone near."

A crackly male voice came back through the radio. "You've not found the escaped prisoner?"

"Escaped prisoner?"

"Yeah, we've had an escapee from cell nine-two-one-seven-four. A human."

A moment's silence before the guard with the radio said, "No, sir, there's nothing here. If there were a human, I'd be able to smell their stink. Vile creatures."

As slowly as he could, Seb backed away from the grate. If one of them looked up, they'd see him for sure. With his breath still held, Seb eased back an inch at a time, and the very slightest *whoosh* sounded out as his clothes rubbed against the brushed metal of the shaft. The reek of aluminium smelled almost like blood. The comparison pulled Seb's stomach taut.

With every minute that passed, Seb grew in confidence. They wouldn't hear him this far back. He had to travel backwards because of how he'd ended up in the shaft, and he didn't have the space to turn around.

As he picked up his pace, each join in the shaft became a sharp shock because he couldn't anticipate what he couldn't see. Seb let his breaths go more than before. The sooner he found a way out of these shafts, the better.

Seb worked up a good pace, moving backwards like he'd been oiled up. The ridges might have hurt when he passed over them, but Seb could also use them to propel himself backwards.

After his hardest push yet, Seb shot along the ventilation shaft like a bar of wet soap down a slide. Before he had time to react, his feet dropped down a hole. In a blink, his legs followed them, pulling his body weight down.

Although he reached out, his hands slapping against the side of the shaft with a wet *boom*, he'd picked up too much momentum and couldn't get a grip.

Used to slow motion in a crisis, everything happened at double the speed this time, and before Seb could gather his thoughts, his stomach hit the roof of his mouth and he fell into the unknown.

Chapter Twenty-Nine

A tugging roused Seb. Something pulled on him like a dog trying to drag a tree root from the ground. Despite his near delirium, he had the presence of mind to keep a hold of the tiny computer and pulled it tightly to his chest.

When Seb opened his eyes, he found Sparks on top of him, her teeth clenched as she clasped both hands to her computer and tried to pry it from his grasp. Before he'd really thought about it, Seb kicked out and knocked the small woman away from him. His world spun when he sat up, and a sharp twinge ran up his back. A deep throb set fire to his left hip, and he could taste his own blood.

After the whack, Sparks cowered away from Seb, and Seb looked up at the chute he'd fallen down. The chimney ran so high he couldn't see the top of it for darkness. The action of looking up wedged spears into the base of his neck, and although Seb shifted from side to side to try to ease the pain, it gave him little relief. With the tiny computer still in his grip, he stood up from the cold metal floor and took several breaths to ride out the agony from the fall. He looked at Sparks. "Where are we?"

"The control room," she said, her bottom lip poked out as a petulant child would. "Now give me my computer back."

Wires came from everywhere and ran along the walls. They all gathered together in the middle and ran into what looked like an electronic brain. A multicoloured mess of flex in the base of it like a spinal cord, the huge brain hung suspended in the middle of the room.

"The entire ship is controlled from here. If we can mess with this, we can lower the ship's defences long enough to get out."

"We? So we're a team now, are we?"

With an outstretched hand, her fingers the length of Seb's forearms, Sparks smiled, her purple eyes aglow in the dark. "We are if you give me my computer back."

"I need something from you first."

A limp jaw and vacant eyes met Seb's request.

"My dad's necklace."

"I don't have it."

"That's a shame."

"What?"

"I said that's a shame. Without my dad's necklace, I'm afraid you ain't getting your computer."

"You'd jeopardise everything to get your dad's necklace back?"

"Yep."

"So we're going to remain prisoners on this ship for the sake of a piece of tin."

"It ain't a piece of tin, and you and I both know it."

"I don't have it."

Seb kept a hold of Sparks' computer. "I suppose we just need to wait here until we get caught, then."

After she'd looked over her shoulder at the door and back to Seb several times, Sparks tutted. "Fine." She pulled the necklace from her pocket. "Here, have it." She threw it at Seb.

Seb caught it. "Useless piece of tin, eh?"

Without another word, Sparks walked over to him and snatched her computer away.

As the small girl tapped against the screen of her computer, Seb got to his feet and walked around the cramped room. Other than the electronic brain in the centre, the place had walls lined with computers and servers. "How do you know we won't crash if you shut everything down?"

Without looking up, her long fingers moving so fast over the screen they were a blur, Sparks shrugged. "I don't."

Seb stared at her to see if she meant it. A heavy frown and no hint of mirth suggested she did. "Great."

It seemed awfully convenient that Sparks had been in the control room when he fell into it. But just before Seb could ask her how she got there, a loud *thunk* ran through the entire ship. The poor lighting in the room got even worse as the emergency lights switched on and cast the place in a red hue.

A loud alarm pulsed through the ship and the door to the control room slid open.

With wide eyes, Sparks looked at Seb while she tucked her computer into her jacket and said, "This is it. We need to go now!"

Chapter Thirty

The siren pulsed as a wet throb that rang so loud it both hurt Seb's ears and upset his balance. It didn't seem to bother Sparks, who sprinted from the control room out into the corridor.

With the electronics blown, the ship had fallen into a safe mode that cast the entire vessel in a deep red glow. The warm light pulsed in time with the alarm. Not quite a strobe light, the dimming and brightening of the red glare hurt Seb's eyes and sent his head into a spin. Every time it darkened, the rapid Sparks vanished from his line of sight. At any moment, Seb expected for the ship to return from darkness and for Sparks to be gone.

Fast for her size, Sparks sped through the corridors. Seb fought to keep up and ran with all he had, his tight lungs fit to burst. Every time the ship went dark, he winced in anticipation of clattering into something. The wrong kind of fall and he wouldn't be getting off *The Black Hole*.

The prisoners seemed to realise at the same time that their cells couldn't contain them. Doors opened all around Seb, and the corridors became swamped with all manner of beings. They obscured Seb's view of Sparks even more. When he caught sight of her, he saw her small frame weaving through the chaos without missing a step as if guided by an innate sense.

Up ahead, Seb saw two prisoners of the same species. Huge red things, they had massive snapping jaws and were both holding up a prison guard. One had the guard's head and shoulders and one had the guard's legs. Not that Seb liked the prison guards in this place, but the way the prisoners looked at the guard, and the guard's helpless struggle, sank cold dread through Seb's guts. Sparks ran through the low archway created by the horizontal guard.

The polished metal floor shone and reflected the red light. Seb dove onto his front and used the low-friction mirrored surface to slide beneath the guard too.

Once back on his feet, a thick and wet ripping sound squelched through the corridor. When Seb looked back, he saw the guard had been torn in two, his insides hanging down and dripping in blood. The corridor around them glistened with the guard's fluids. Thank God he'd gotten through before that happened.

With Sparks at the edge of where he could see, Seb fought against his tired body and pushed on, shoving the prisoners aside as he barged through after the little rat. If she ran away without helping him …

As the light grew in brightness again, Seb saw Sparks had stopped in front of a door. The glow of her computer screen lit up her face as she stared down at it. When Seb closed the distance, he nearly laughed. In any other situation, he would have.

Once he arrived at the door, he grabbed the handle, which sat too high for Sparks to reach, and opened the door for her. Although she didn't say anything, Sparks looked up at Seb, an irked expression on her small face.

The door led to what looked like a maintenance shaft. Dark like the rest of the ship, it too pulsed with the red light that made everything so difficult to see. Stairs led both up and down.

With Sparks still locked on her computer screen, Seb looked at the carnage in the corridor behind them before he closed the door on more prisoners taking over the prison. Just before he shut it, a guard screamed as he fell to a barrage of blows. "Which way, Sparks?"

After a couple more seconds of staring at her screen, the diminutive Sparks lifted her head and pointed down the stairs. "That way."

***

Sparks took off again, leaving Seb in her wake. She ran down three flights of stairs before she stopped beside another door with a high handle.

When Seb caught up, he gasped for breath as the small woman pointed at it. "We need to go through there. There's escape pods on this level and the next one down. If we can activate one, we can get out of here."

The girl hadn't broken a sweat. Exhausted from trying to keep up with her, Seb had stars in his vision from his ragged breaths. After one final gasp, he reached the high door handle and pushed the door open.

The collection of guards on the other side turned as one. A

quick count and Seb saw six of them, and they all stared at him and Sparks. "Damn it," Seb said as he pulled the door back to hide behind it. He managed to close it in time for it to act as a shield against the first rush of blaster fire.

When Seb looked around, he saw Sparks had taken off again and heard her light footsteps tap the metal stairs as she ran down to the next floor. Seb followed her down.

This time the door had a chair next to it, which Sparks used to reach the handle. She shoved the door open and ran through. Seb followed after her.

The sound of Seb's clumsy footsteps echoed in the narrow metal corridor, and Sparks opened up another lead on him. They'd obviously found a part of the ship with no prisoners because the tight tunnel stood empty. Good job. The girl already had the beating of him; he didn't need any more obstructions.

Clearly not at a full sprint, yet faster than Seb, Sparks rushed ahead and stared at her computer as she ran. With the alarm as a disorientating throb through his skull, Seb chased after her. The last person on the planet he would have trusted before now, Seb had put his life in the small creature's large hands.

As they rounded a bend, they came to three hatches for escape pods. Sparks arrived at one of them and pulled on the door. When she looked back at Seb, her wide purple eyes spread wider. "It's locked."

"Well, open it, then," Seb said.

With her attention on her computer, she shook her head as her fingers danced across the screen. "I can't! I need to hack it."

The stampede of what must have been the guards they'd left

on the floor above them beat a tattoo against the steel floor of the corridor as they closed in on the pair.

Seb looked behind but couldn't see them for the kink in the passageway. "You *need* to hurry up."

"You're going to need to buy me some time, Seb."

A deep breath did little for Seb's tight lungs, but he had no choice. When he turned around to go back to the guards, he shook his head. "I knew this was a bad idea."

Before he rounded the bend, Seb did all he could to level himself out. Six guards, he'd have to bring his A-game to beat them. One final breath and Seb stepped around the corner.

Chapter Thirty-One

Six creatures faced him—all of them ugly, all of them a different species, and all of them larger than Seb. Even the smallest of the pack stood a good head and shoulders above him. As one, they raised their blasters and pointed them at him.

The world around Seb dropped into slow motion and he ran at them.

The red lasers from the blasters flew, each one travelling much quicker than the fists he'd grown used to fighting. With the pain of the last blaster fire still in his left ear, Seb dodged the first wave, moving like a flamenco dancer with his contorted twists and turns. At least, that was how it felt. He probably looked more like a geriatric one step away from falling flat on his face.

When Seb got close to the first guard, he jumped at a wall, kicked off from it, and used it to propel himself forward. He led with a clenched fist. Like most creatures, the guard had a weak spot on its chin. When Seb connected with the scaled and leathered skin of the monster, its head snapped to the side with a wet slap and its eyes rolled back.

As it fell, Seb moved onto the second creature. With his focus on the second guard's chest, Seb jumped again and drove a kick into where her heart was. The impact forced the wind from her with an *oomph*. The stench of her breath nearly broke Seb's focus. She smelled like she ate her own waste. The guard flew backwards into the others before she collapsed to the ground.

As the others found their bearings, Seb jumped over the second downed guard and drove two quick jabs to the faces of the next two. They both folded like wet paper.

Seb caught their blasters, one in each hand, and let off two shots at the remaining guards. Each shot scored a hit. Like in the sewers, he hit them in the legs. Enough to halt their progress, but not enough to kill them.

The pair rolled in agony on the floor as Seb closed in on them. He punched the first one in the temple and it instantly went limp.

As Seb stood over the last of the six, he looked down at it. A Mandulu, it stared up at Seb. The speed of Seb's world returned to normal and he said, "Welcome to nature's anaesthetic." He kicked the dumb being square in the chin. A wet crack and the thing turned floppy like all of the others had. With his jaw clenched, Seb stared down at the monster, resisting the urge to hit it again. They needed to get out of there regardless of his desire to inflict pain on the dumb beast.

As he picked his way back through the six downed guards, Seb fought for breath. Each one lay unconscious on the floor, breathing but not moving. A quick glance to check none would get up again and Seb ran back toward Sparks.

When he came around the bend, he heard the *whoosh* of boosters. A glance out of one of the porthole windows and he saw a tiny pod shoot from the ship. His entire being sank. Sparks had left him behind.

Chapter Thirty-Two

With his fists balled so tightly he dug his nails into his palms, Seb clenched his jaw to keep himself from shouting. It would serve no purpose for him to rage. Now he'd been left on the ship, he simply needed to find somewhere to hide. With the escape pod turning into a dot as it shot away from *The Black Hole*, Seb shook his head and breathed heavily through his nose. Of course the rat would screw him over at some point. Seb had been an idiot to trust her. Sure, he had his dad's necklace back, but a fat lot of good that would do when he got caught and locked up again. They'd probably process him sooner than thirty days now just to make an example of him.

On his way down the corridor, Seb broke into a jog. The escape pod that had been fired had a red light above its closed door. However, the light above the one next to it remained green and the door hung open. Hope lifted in Seb's chest. He could still get off *The Black Hole*. Maybe Sparks wanted to go her own way, but at least she'd given him an escape too.

When he arrived at the unused pod, slightly out of breath from the run, he peered into the tiny vessel to see the wide purple eyes and wonky grin of Sparks staring straight back at him.

"Hi," she said.

"I … I thought you'd—"

"Left you? No, not yet at least. Sure, you're annoying, but not so annoying that I'd leave you in the lurch."

As Seb stepped into the small pod, he rolled his eyes at her comment.

"Did you take out all of the guards?" Sparks asked.

"Yep. They won't be getting up again anytime soon."

Sparks made room for Seb to sit down and pressed a series of buttons. The door hissed as it closed on them. Not quite crushed—another body and they would have been for sure—Seb and Sparks sat hunched up in the small space.

"So why did you send out an empty escape pod?"

"If anyone's watching for escapees, I wanted to give them something to focus their attention on. I thought it would give us the best chance of getting away unnoticed. If we'd had more time, I would have sent them all out. It's much easier to hide when you're one of many."

The tiny pod shook, and Seb laughed as he sat back in his seat. As much as he wanted to knock the little rat out, she saw angles Seb hadn't even considered. Something still struck Seb as odd. This whole meeting seemed far too convenient. "Sparks, how did you get out of your cell?"

Numbers counted down on the small screen in front of Sparks, who didn't seem to hear Seb as she focused on them.

3 …

2 …

1.

The pod wobbled and rattled, forcing Seb to reach out and steady himself by grabbing onto a handle inside the tight space. A few seconds later and it shook so much, it rocked Seb's vision. Such a tight grip, it hurt Seb's knuckles as he held on with all he had. The pod then punched away from the ship and spun off into space.

Chapter Thirty-Three

Despite the parachute to slow them down, the escape pod hurtled toward the ground of the planet they'd set their sights on like it would bore straight through to the core. Sparks said she didn't know anything about the place; she just picked one of the several closest planets she could find to get them away from *The Black Hole*. They'd not managed to say much else to one another as the pod whooshed along.

Seconds before they crashed down, Seb locked a tighter grip on the handrails inside the pod. His stomach lifted into his throat, and his palms ran damp with sweat.

They collided with the ground with an almighty *boom*. The shake ran through the entire pod and threw Seb across it. He crashed into the opposite wall and his vision tilted like he'd pass out.

As the pod skimmed over the ground like a flat stone over a lake, each jolt, though diminished from the one before it, tossed Seb around the pod. Sparks, who gripped onto the railing like Seb had tried to, somehow managed to remain in the same place the entire time.

Once the pod finally rolled to a halt, Seb sighed and fell back, his entire body aching from the beating he'd just taken inside the small vessel.

Unable to move, he watched Sparks jump to her feet. "How the hell did you manage to stay in the same spot?"

"We may be small," Sparks said as she kicked the door away from the pod. The heavy metal cover hit the solid ground with a *clang*. "But we know how to ride out a crash landing. As a species, we make a habit of quick getaways."

A wind—so bitter it gave Seb a sinus headache—rushed into the escape pod when Sparks jumped out of the doorway. The aggressive cold rush of air kick-started Seb to life, and he too jumped up and clambered out of the small spherical vessel.

Sparks had already taken shelter from the wind behind a rock, so Seb joined her. The ground they stood on, although dark, could also be seen through; it looked almost like black glass. The chill in the air ran straight to Seb's bones. As he stood out of the wind, he shivered and looked down. Veins of deep red ran through the rocks. "Is that—?"

"Lava?" Sparks called back at him, shouting over the wind.

"Yeah."

"It sure looks like it, doesn't it?"

"But it's so cold."

"Maybe the planet's external temperature stops it getting any higher than this? The cold wind must be what makes this planet habitable."

A stamp on the ground showed Seb just how solid the surface was. "How curious."

"So what do we do now?" Sparks said.

"Huh?"

With her wide purple eyes fixed on him, Sparks spoke long and slow words. "Well … we've completed phase one: escape from the prison ship. Now we're on a hostile planet, so what do we do?"

From where they stood, Seb could see *The Black Hole* up in the sky. As he looked at it, he laughed. "I bet it's chaos up there at the moment. They're going to be wanting us more than ever now."

When he looked at Sparks, he saw her mouth open and head tilted back as she too looked up at the ship.

"I think we should move on as quickly as possible," Seb said. Before Sparks could respond, he climbed up on top of the rock they'd chosen to hide behind.

The strong wind nearly knocked Seb off, and he shielded his eyes with his hand to look over at the lights in the distance. "I think …" He paused. The same vacant expression remained fixed on Sparks' face. She clearly couldn't hear a word he said up there.

Seb jumped down and landed with a jolt that snapped through him. "There are lights over that way. It must be a spaceport. I think we need to find a cargo ship that we can sneak onto so we can go to another planet. I mean, how long will it be before they track the homing beacon in the escape pod?"

"A long time."

Seb waited for Sparks to elaborate.

"I disabled the homing beacon. Although, not on the first pod. They'll be looking for that one before they even think to look for us. And I sent that to a different planet."

An urge to hug the strange little genius took over Seb, but he refrained. It would be far too awkward. Besides, the little rat robbed him the last time they hugged. She might have got them off *The Black Hole*, but she needed to do a lot more than that to gain Seb's trust.

As Sparks adjusted her glasses, she grinned. "I reckon we'll be okay to rest up for the night before we move on."

A sharp nod of his head, his body still alive with the aches of their crash landing, and Seb said, "Okay. That sounds like a plan."

Without another word, Sparks tapped her tiny computer and it lit up like a powerful torch. A quick sweep of their environment and she stopped a few seconds later to highlight the huge cave just in front of them. The cave didn't stand high above ground level, which was why they hadn't noticed it in the dark, but it went down deep, by the looks of things. "That's got to be as good a place as any, right?"

A choice of words that Seb wouldn't have ever used, but it seemed to be the only place they had. Instead of being negative, he remained quiet and followed Sparks into the mouth of the huge cave.

Chapter Thirty-Four

Once Seb had entered the cave with Sparks, he stared into the darkness beyond. The torch on her small computer proved utterly ineffective against the complete absence of light before them. Although the red veins of lava ran through the cold ground away from them, they provided no guide to travel by, just a warning of how deep they would plunge into the darkness should they choose to go farther.

For a few seconds, neither Seb nor Sparks spoke as they stared into the void. Seb clenched his jaw tightly against the cold onslaught of the wind that cannoned through the place, and he gulped. "How far back do you think it goes?"

Instead of a reply, Sparks shot an arm out and grabbed a hold of Seb's right bicep in a tight grip.

It spiked Seb's pulse as the small being dragged him down into a hunch, and she clung on so tight, it stung where her fingers dug in. As Seb's eyes adjusted to the light, more of the cave became clear to him. Not far from where they crouched sat a dense line of growths that looked like a cross between trees and stalagmites. Impossible to tell how far back they went, they spread across the width of the cave as a line of soldiers would when protecting a fort.

Before Seb could speak, he finally saw what Sparks had seen. The creature moved among the tree-mites, seemingly oblivious to its hungry observers. A dark form, slightly darker than the cave, the quadruped dipped its head once or twice to sniff the ground. Were it to stand on its hind legs, the creature would have been taller than Seb. Not quite the size of a horse, it stood larger than even the biggest dog he'd ever seen. "What is it?" Seb said.

At first Sparks didn't reply. The creature tensed at the sound of Seb's voice. Once it settled down again, Sparks finally spoke in a whisper. "Not sure, but whatever it is, it looks more edible than the slop they fed us on *The Black Hole*."

Until that moment, Seb had only been able to slip into slow motion when a fight came to him. As he turned his attention inward, the sides of his vision blurred and the creature stood out among everything else. The space between its eyes stood prominent for Seb.

With slow and deliberate steps, Seb moved toward the creature, his fists clenched, his breathing slow. So dark in the cave, Seb could almost feel the absence of light against his skin. When he came to the first row of tree-like growths, he paused for a moment before he delved deeper into their shadowed embrace.

The creature seemed oblivious to Seb's approach as he made his way closer on tiptoes. When he got to within a few feet, he stepped on a twig. Even in slow motion, the creature's head snapped up and focused on him. The brown orbs that were its eyes widened, but it had no more time to react as Seb darted forward and punched it in the forehead.

Like everything he punched, the creature fell. Several more of the large brown quadrupeds burst from the darkness before they plunged deeper into it. How had he not seen any of them?

Sparks flashed past Seb and jumped onto the beast he'd knocked down as she plunged a knife into its skull. The brown velveteen creature's back legs kicked out behind it before it fell limp.

"How did you get a knife?" Seb asked her. "And how did you manage to keep a hold of my necklace when they locked you up?"

Instead of answering him, Sparks stared down at the dead beast and said, "Come on then." She lifted its legs and made out like she wanted to drag it along, but the thing must have been three times her weight at least. "I don't know what's down in the darkness of this cave, but I want to get away from it before I have a chance to find out."

She had a point. Seb grabbed the large creature around its hooves and dragged it closer to the entrance of the cave. They found a spot where the wall met the ground, an alcove that offered some protection from the wind. The glassy floor might have been hard and cold, but it made dragging something at least twice his weight much easier than it otherwise would have been.

With her knife still in her hand, Sparks stuck the creature and tore a line down its skin. "You go and get something we can burn and I'll skin this thing. See if you can get a spit as well, yeah?"

How dare she tell him what to do?! Although, as Seb watched Sparks peel back the first layer of the creature's skin, he saw that her skill outweighed his pride. He shrugged and walked into the trees; collecting wood had to be better than what she currently faced.

***

Although not wood, the tree-like growths might as well have been. Seb returned with an armful of branches in varying shapes and sizes from the strange things, all of them dry. When he dropped them on the hard ground, each one clattered with its own pitch. When Seb sat down, the cold and hard surface felt instantly uncomfortable beneath his seat and his bottom turned numb. When hunger rumbled through his stomach, Seb did his best to ignore the discomfort of the ground and arranged the sticks so he could light a fire.

Once he'd piled them up, the larger sticks on the bottom and the smaller ones on top, he handed Sparks a snapped-off branch.

"What's this?" she said.

"The best we've got. You're going to have to use it to cook with. I have one too. If we spear the meat, we can hang it over the flames."

Although Sparks looked sceptical, she didn't voice her doubt. Good job, really. She wouldn't have been able to do any better than he just had.

"Okay," Sparks said, "stand back."

As Seb moved away from the newly built fire, Sparks lifted up her tiny computer and held it to the wood. When she pressed her finger to the screen, a small spark burst from it and landed amongst the pile of sticks. Several more presses sent several more sparks into it until they glowed collectively.

Seb leaned forward and blew on them while Sparks continued to skin the creature. In between breaths, he pulled away from the smoke and looked at the girl. "Is there anything that computer doesn't do?"

After she'd wiped the sweat from her brow with the back of her forearm, her hands glistening with the creature's dark blood, Sparks said, "It doesn't skin animals."

Seb half-laughed before he returned to blowing on the fire.

***

The meat, cooked well enough to eat, tasted rich and gamey. A million times better than anything Seb had had in the prison—or on Aloo for that matter. As Seb chewed on the huge chunk he'd bitten off, he looked around the cave. With so many red veins of lava, the place looked like the insides of some great creature, almost like they'd found their way into its lungs. Were it not for the same effect running through the ground outside the cave, Seb wouldn't have entertained the idea of coming inside. But from what little experience they'd had with the frigid and rocky planet, the entire place looked this way.

After he'd swallowed a large chunk of meat, Seb looked over at Sparks. "So tell me about yourself."

Sparks looked up mid-chew. "Huh?"

"Well, why are you such a scheming little rat? There must be a reason for it."

Although Sparks shot him a glare, she didn't deny his

accusation. Instead, she lowered the meat from her mouth and took a deep breath. "I was orphaned at a young age."

For the first time since he'd met her, Seb found some emotion beneath her cold exterior in the way her voice shook when she spoke. "I'm sorry," he said.

"Now, being an orphan in this galaxy is hard enough, but being an orphan where I'm from is hell."

"Where are you from?"

"A planet called Thryst. It's stuck in the last millennia and still uses living beings to run most of its industries. Although, they don't take the jobs willingly because they don't pay that well, and once you get into them, you never leave. So they use institutionalised people as, essentially, slaves—prisoners and orphans mainly. Because of this, you can't fart on Thryst without getting arrested, and once they have you in front of a court, they throw the book at you. Of all of the galaxy's prisoners, twenty-five percent of them are on Thryst. That's over sixty percent of all living beings on our planet. Soon the place will be nothing but a prison planet, the perfect, low-cost workforce. The people who run the place get fat off its exports. At twelve, I recognised that if I went to the authorities for help, I'd never leave the system. I didn't want to be a slave like so many of my species."

With a deep frown, Seb sighed. "Wow. What a lot to have to deal with. And what a crappy planet."

"Tell me about it."

"So what did you do?"

"I lived on the streets. On the first night something ..." Sparks broke off and looked down at her lap. Her bottom lip stuck out as she drew a stuttered breath. When she finally looked back up, her purple eyes were glazed and she spoke through clenched teeth. "Let's just say something happened, shall we? Something happened that will never happen to me again."

Nausea locked Seb's stomach tight and he remained silent so Sparks could continue.

"The second night I broke into an abandoned building and locked the place behind me. I managed to sleep and get out of there again before morning. After that day, I learned pretty fast how to break in and out of places. I would rob people, bust into abandoned buildings to sleep, and play tricks on some of the powerful people on Thryst just because I could." With her computer glowing on the ground, she nodded down at it. "When I learned how to use that thing, I became unstoppable."

The little sociopath suddenly made sense to Seb. To survive on her own from such a young age, she had to be able to switch off her feelings.

"So," Sparks said, "it's hard for me to trust anyone now, you know?"

"That's why you steal?"

"I see beings as things I can take from, and that's all. Although"—she looked up at Seb again, her large purple eyes glistening with tears—"you're starting to show me another way. I'm sorry I robbed you, I really am."

A gentle nod, and Seb reached up to his dad's necklace just to be sure she hadn't taken it again. "It's fine. Now I understand where you're coming from, it's a little easier to bear. We can draw a line through it and start again. Besides, you didn't have to wait for me in the escape pod on *The Black Hole*, so I figure we're more than even now."

After another bite of her steak, Sparks nodded. "Thank you for understanding."

Chapter Thirty-Five

"So, Sebastian, what about you?"

"If you call me Sebastian again …" When Seb looked at Sparks' crooked smile, the tension left his face and he laughed. She was not an easy one to stay angry with; he shook his head and adjusted how he sat so a different part of his body took its turn at bearing the brunt of the cold wind.

"I have a brother," Seb said. "He's in prison."

"What for?"

"He used to be a cop. Then he got into a fight and killed someone. It made it even worse that he was a cop, so they threw the book at him. Life without parole. I'll never see him again."

"You don't visit?"

"He won't let us. Said he doesn't want to be reminded of the mistakes he's made."

Sparks lowered her head. "That's sad."

"I know, right?"

"Doesn't he know that you still love him?"

"Well, the thing is, I'm not sure my dad did. He used to be a cop too and raised us like we were borderline criminals. Like we'd go over the edge at any point. Especially since Mum died. He wasn't the best communicator in the world. We had a difficult relationship, so when my brother messed up, it kind of felt like he'd fulfilled my dad's prophecy."

"You say 'had' when you talk about your dad. Is he not about now?"

A shake of his head and Seb looked out into the darkness behind him. He studied the veins of red that ran through the rock. They looked like they stretched forever, and maybe tiredness affected his perception, but as he stared at them, he could have sworn they pulsed. "He died just a few years ago."

"I'm sorry."

"I'm not sure I am. I did feel sad for a while, but if I'm honest, it felt like a relief to have him gone. When Mum died, it left a huge hole in our lives. The heart of the family seemed to perish with her. I was only ten at the time and I needed someone to put their arm around my shoulder and tell me—" The grief snuck up on Seb and stopped him in his tracks. He cleared his throat. "—that they loved me. Dad wasn't that kind of guy, you know? So from a very young age, I always felt alone. Like I'd have to work it out myself. Dad came in with advice, well, Dad criticised me from time to time, but other than that, he didn't have anything useful to offer. As sons, we both disappointed him. One of my regrets is that I never got to tell him how much he disappointed me as a father. The guy let me down. Although, I did tell him the wrong parent died when we had an argument once."

Sparks gasped. "Wow. Do you regret that?"

"I wish I did. I'm not sure I care anymore." When Seb

looked up, tired from opening his heart to Sparks, he saw her crying freely. It shocked him how she'd managed to keep it from her tone. "I'm sorry. Too much information, right?"

A shake of her head and Sparks spoke through her tears. "No, don't be sorry. Thank you for telling me. I always wished one of my parents had survived. I wanted a parent to help me grieve, but hearing your story …" Sparks broke down again.

Seb drew a deep breath, blinked away his tears, and lifted his head. When he looked back at Sparks, he said, "I think it's about time I slept."

Sparks nodded.

"Night, Sparks."

"Night, Seb."

Once Seb had lain down on the hard and cold ground, he curled up into the foetal position and stared at the fire's burning embers. He drew a stuttered breath. If only he could see his mum one last time.

Chapter Thirty-Six

By the time Seb woke up, the coldness from the glassy rock he'd slept on had permeated his entire being. Although he looked at the mouth of the cave and saw daylight, he shivered from how little warmth it brought with it.

Gripped from head to toe with aches, from his fall and fights on board *The Black Hole* to his escape and bedding down on the hard ground of the cave, Seb remained still as he stared at the smouldering mound they'd used to cook the creature on yesterday. Unlike normal trees, the stuff they'd built the fire with the previous evening seemed to burn forever. The rich taste of the gamey beast lay as a fur on Seb's tongue, and it seemed that no amount of dry swallows would rid his mouth of the funk.

When he finally found the strength to sit up, a pain spasmed through his neck. One wrong move and he'd be locked in agony for days.

As he slowly adjusted his position, cautious in how he let his body unwind an inch at a time, Seb looked for the carcass of the animal they'd eaten the previous night. Most of it would remain uncooked, but the night sure as hell remained cold enough that the meat would have stayed edible. Before anything, they should cook it up so they had something to take with them. Except …

"Sparks," Seb said.

Although she fixed him with her large purple eyes, her facial expression existed as a snapshot. When Seb leaned close to her, he heard gentle snoring. Seb stared at the small creature for a moment, his jaw slightly loose as he watched the unique way she slept. Her glassy stare made her look dead. A chill snapped through him and he nudged her to banish the creepy vision and spoke a little louder. "Sparks."

The girl twitched before she blinked repeatedly. She stretched her arms and legs out as if to force her hands and feet as far away from one another as she possibly could. Her voice croaked when she said, "What is it?"

"Where's the rest of the animal we ate last night?"

But Sparks didn't answer. Instead, she sat bolt upright and looked around. She scratched her head, her black bob lacking its usual sharpness from where she'd slept on it. She finally looked back at Seb and made a noncommittal, "Huh?"

Despite the daylight, Seb still couldn't see the back of their cave. The veins of lava ran away from them, beneath the line of trees just twenty or so metres away, and into the void beyond.

When Sparks stood up, Seb did too. Her sharp gasp snapped through the enclosed space and dove down into the darkness of the tree-mites. "Do you see …?" she said.

"Yep, I do." Seb fought against the wobble in his voice as he said, "What the hell?"

A pool of blood lay from where they'd dumped the creature

the previous evening. That seemed fairly normal. However, the trail that led away from it, from where the creature had been dragged off, made Seb's skin turn to gooseflesh.

When Sparks lit up the torch on her computer, it revealed a long and wet line that ran away from them. "Probably just another animal, I'd say." Although she sounded far from convinced.

"Yeah, I'd say so too. I mean, life has to be hard on this rocky planet. There's probably plenty of opportunists around." Before Sparks could respond, Seb added, "Whatever it was, we need to move on. We need to find a spaceport and get out of here."

Seb faced the daylight outside the cave and walked toward it.

The patter of Sparks' feet caught up with him and she fell into stride beside him. The pair said nothing to one another as they quickly marched from the place. What could they say? That something big enough to drag a creature heavier than Seb came up while they slept and pulled it away. Anything could have happened to them.

At the mouth of the cave, Seb walked outside and peered across at what looked like a spaceport in the distance. The wind had picked up and blew stronger than the previous night. Not only did the bitter gales cut to his bones, but they burned his skin. As Seb wrapped himself in a tight hug, he looked at Sparks and the breath left his lungs. "You're bleeding."

When she looked back, her hair tossed by the strong gusts, she drew a sharp breath. "You are too."

After he'd wiped his hand down the side of his face, Seb looked at his palm to see it had turned red. "Damn, what do you ..." But before he could finish, Sparks raised her palm into the wind.

A few seconds later she turned it to face Seb. It too ran red with her blood. "It's the wind," she said. "There's something in the wind that's cutting us. Almost like glass."

Sparks ducked back into the cave and Seb followed.

Once inside the cave, Seb's face throbbed from what felt like a thousand paper cuts. Another rub of his skin and he found more blood on his hands. "We can't go back out there again. It may be a storm, or it may be the daylight that does it to the planet's atmosphere. We'll have to sit and wait it out."

Although Sparks opened her mouth to speak, a breeze rushed up the cave, a breeze warmer than the one outside. It cut her dead as both she and Seb stared into the darkness below.

"Did you feel that?" Sparks said.

"Yep."

"This isn't a cave, is it, Seb?"

Seb shook his head.

"What do you think?"

"Huh?"

"We could go through here."

Another shake of his head and Seb said, "What about the thing that dragged the animal off? That's down there."

"It'll be long gone. If it didn't wake us, then it's probably more scared of us than we are of it."

When Seb squinted into the darkness again, he saw just how far the veins stretched away from them. "I suppose it has to lead somewhere, right?" he said. "The breeze wouldn't come from a dead end."

"It's gotta be better than standing here while we wait for something to change. We need to get off this planet before they send a search party down here, so I'd rather do something than nothing. We've got my torch to guide us." At that moment, Sparks started up her computer and tapped at the screen. After she'd brought an image of a planet up, she turned the screen to Seb and said, "Look."

"What am I looking at?"

"This is the planet we're on."

Seb squinted to read the writing on the screen. "Zenk."

Another tap of the screen brought up a video of the planet's surface, and Sparks said, "It says here that the glass winds continue unabated all day, every day. Daylight can last for up to sixteen of their twenty hours, and nothing survives outside during the day."

Another look into the total darkness of the cave and Seb looked back at the image of the planet they currently stood on. After a deep breath, he nodded. "Okay. Let's do this."

Chapter Thirty-Seven

As Seb got closer to the line of tree-mites with Sparks at his side, he looked down at the thin streams of red beneath his feet. With each step down, he expected the ground to warm up, but the temperature never changed. The cold, glassy environment remained as frigid and hostile as ever.

Sparks kept the torch on her computer on, which lit up the ground and the line of blood from where the creature's carcass had been dragged away from them while they slept.

"What do you think took it?" Seb asked when he saw Sparks stare at the mess again.

Without lifting her head, Sparks raised her torch to light up more of the trail. "I'm not sure. I just hope this tunnel brings us out closer to the spaceport and off this hideous planet. Is it too much to ask for a bit of greenery, air that doesn't cut us to shreds, and an existence where I don't have to live in fear of something eating us? Add to that that we have beings that want to imprison us for no reason whatsoever."

'No reason whatsoever' seemed a little naive—Seb had beaten up too many people to count, and Sparks had robbed her way through Aloo. But he didn't say anything; the mood in the cave didn't need to go any darker.

With the tree-mites packed so tightly together, their roots mixed in with the glassy rock and the veins of lava, Seb negotiated his way through by holding the rough bark of one before he moved onto the next. He might not have been able to see his way, but at least he could feel it.

When Seb stepped forward another pace, something cold and leathery sprang from the darkness. It slapped him in the face from being startled to life. Seb's heart exploded as the creature smothered him in a panicked and flapping frenzy before it knocked him over.

A dull thud jolted through Seb's body when he hit the hard ground. He pulled the creature off him, and it took flight. It disappeared into the dark while Seb lay panting on the floor.

When Sparks lifted her torch, Seb's heart leapt in his chest. Above them, in the branches of the tree-mites, hung hundreds of creatures. Like large exotic fruit, they hung down, their wings wrapped around their bodies like cocoons. The average size of the beasts ran around a metre in length and Seb's skin crawled to look at them. If they all took off at the same time … he shuddered.

So preoccupied with the creatures and darkness, Seb hadn't noticed the damp and tacky ground … until he put his hands in it. Sat amongst the mess, he looked around to see the layer of excrement they'd been wading through. What he'd taken to be loam of some sort turned out to be the waste of the winged creatures above. Apparently odourless, the sticky layer felt like milky snot to touch.

Seb jumped to his feet and rubbed his hands against his trousers.

When he looked up, he found Sparks staring at him. "Are you okay?"

Sore and covered in crap, Seb's face flushed hot. "I'm fine. Come on, let's go."

***

After about ten minutes, they came out of the other side of the tree-mites. A deep ache sat in Seb's back from having to walk with a stoop to avoid the creatures, and his calves stung from walking on tiptoes to keep the noise down. Any sound could have startled them, and the thought of them all taking flight at the same time spun Seb out.

Although darker than before, Seb breathed more easily in the vast open space on the other side of the tree-mites. From the look of the glowing red trails in the rock, the ground beneath them ran on a steep decline into the tunnel.

"I'm not sure I like this," Sparks said as she held her torch out. The beam shook at the end of her outstretched arm.

"Anything's got to be better than going back the way we came," Seb replied.

The torch beam swung around as Sparks lit up the tree-mites behind them and the creatures in them. She didn't reply as she seemed to consider her options.

"Let me put it another way," Seb said. "I'm going down into this tunnel now. I'm not prepared to debate it, and if I have to go on my own, then I will. However, I'd rather you came with me."

Before Sparks could reply, Seb walked off down the hill. A few seconds later, the beam from Sparks' computer followed him. Thank God. He needed both the light and the company more than he'd been prepared to say.

***

The farther they plunged into the darkness, the steeper the decline. "If we're not careful," Sparks said, "this could turn into a cliff and we could fall to the bottom."

Panting from their descent and sweating profusely, Seb didn't reply. They'd committed to it now; they had to keep going. A deep burn streaked through his legs because of the angle of the drop, but he continued down, and Sparks—despite her tiny form—kept pace with him.

Just when the angle felt like it couldn't get any steeper without them falling over, the ground flattened out.

As Seb stared into the inky void in front of them, he grinned. "See, I told you we'd make it to the bottom." He then added, "You never did tell me how you got out of your cell on *The Black Hole*."

Sparks didn't reply. Instead, she swiped her torch around them.

Seb watched her for a few seconds before he asked, "What are you doing?"

"I don't think we're in a tunnel anymore."

"Huh?"

"It's bigger than a tunnel down here."

"How can you tell?"

"Can't you feel it?"

Seb let the silence hang as he stretched his senses out into the dark environment around them. As much as he wanted to deny what Sparks had just said, he could feel the vastness of the space stretch away from them. Something about it felt infinite like the sky, although they couldn't see any more than a few metres in front of them, the torchlight ineffective in such a large space. Even the veins of lava seemed to be less visible, almost as if they ran deeper than they had up on the surface.

To test the theory, Seb made a noise as loud as he could. "Ooooo-weeeee."

Like an eagle taking flight, the sound of his call rushed away from them. The long drawn-out note seemed to last a lifetime. As Seb waited for an echo to come back to him, his throat dried. The sound died without returning. "I think you're right, Sparks. It seems endless down here."

The light wobbled in Spark's hand and her voice shook. "What shall we do? Where shall we go?"

"Straight."

"Straight?"

"Yep, I think we should continue straight ahead. This room has to end somewhere, right?" To test the vastness of the room again, Seb called once more into the dark. "Ooooooo—weeeeeeee."

The slap of Sparks' hand stung Seb's upper arm and she hissed, "Will you *stop* doing that?"

Before Seb could reply, a noise came back to him. Although not the mimic of his sound that he'd hoped to hear. At first, he heard something like the groaning of a large tree as it fell to years of rot, but the tree didn't land. Instead, it morphed into a deep and vision-shaking roar.

Chapter Thirty-Eight

Panic came at Seb from every angle as he spun on the spot in the darkness and tried to pinpoint the sound. It surrounded him.

When it came again, deep and booming, it sounded so loud it shook the ground beneath Seb's feet. "Those roars sound like they could bring the damn ceiling down."

When Seb looked at Sparks, he saw that she too spun on the spot, her torchlight reaching out away from her, but not spreading far in the darkness. Another look at their surroundings and Seb lost his breath. Such a complete absence of light, in spite of Sparks' torch, it pressed against him as if to suck the vision from his eyes. "Which way were we originally headed?"

Sparks stopped, and for a moment, she stayed silent. Then, in a small voice, she said, "I'm not sure."

A third roar—louder than the previous two—hit Seb like a hard wave and he stumbled backwards, but it helped him pinpoint where the sound came from. With his pulse fluttering like a hummingbird's heart, his breath got away from him. "Whatever way we were headed before"—he stopped to pull himself together—"doesn't matter. All we need to do now is get away from that sound."

Another roar and Sparks took off first.

Seb followed her torchlight, but the gap between him and Sparks increased with every step. As he watched the feeble beam wobble, he gave everything he had to the chase, his chest burning and his pulse throbbing through his temples.

The roar sounded again behind them, loud enough that it echoed through the vast underground amphitheatre as a deep boom. When Seb looked behind, he only saw darkness and the veins of lava that ran through the ground.

In that one look over his shoulder, Sparks seemed to have doubled the distance between them, and her torchlight had dimmed from the increasing gap she opened up between them. Torn between his need to breathe and his desire to call after her, Seb opted to breathe. She'd wait for him … hopefully.

When the solid ground shook beneath Seb's feet, he looked over his shoulder again as he continued to run. What had been dark only moments earlier now took on a new form. Still dark, but Seb saw a silhouette. It stood blacker than its surroundings; almost as if the creature took on a deeper shade than the inky void around it. Nestled in the form sat two flaming eyes—each one's diameter taller than Seb. Glowing orange, the eyes burned like furnaces and they belched grey smoke into the air.

The silhouette shifted to look like the creature had opened its wide mouth. When it drew a deep breath, it dragged Seb's clothes backwards and pulled him toward it. It released a roar again that caused Seb to stumble, and he nearly toppled forward.

The hot rush of air from the creature's mouth reeked of

smoke and it choked Seb. As he fought to breathe, Seb focused on keeping his legs working. His face burned with sweat, and his pulse galloped out of control.

When he looked back in front of him, Sparks had gone.

Chapter Thirty-Nine

Seb opened his mouth to call after Sparks but lost his words when the smoke from the creature's eyes choked him. Every inhalation felt like trying to drag air in through gauze and made Seb's head spin. Dizzy and tired, Seb's world slipped into slow motion. Like the weak spots that opened up before him when he fought, Seb now saw a path he could follow.

Another look behind and the monster had gotten closer. A wall of shadow, it seemed to fill what space Seb could see. Each of its thunderous steps rocked the ground and threw Seb off balance. With his arms windmilling to help him remain upright, Seb kept going.

About thirty seconds passed before Seb turned around again. This time, he had to crane his neck to look up at the creature behind him. Its eyes glowed so bright, they lit up the ceiling above it. At least twenty metres tall, it seemed to stretch as wide. Although Seb couldn't entirely make out where its form finished and the dark started, it didn't matter, many more steps forward and the thing would crush him beneath one of its heavy feet.

When Seb looked in front of him again, everything in slow

motion, he still saw no sign of Sparks, but a path remained visible. No breath left in his lungs to call out, he pushed on, his legs wobbly, his will well and truly shaken.

Then Seb saw it. The glow of the monster's eyes lit up a wall in front of him. Finally, the edge of the open space that contained the creature. The path he saw before him led to a small tunnel that stood about two metres tall. Inside it, he saw the glow of Sparks' torch. If he got to that, the beast on his tail wouldn't have a chance of getting through behind him.

The heavy footfalls had gotten so close to Seb, each one flipped him from the ground like a pea on a drum. As they slammed down behind him, a gust of wind dragged at Seb's clothes, and the next step promised to crush him. The smell of bonfires smothered him, but he kept on.

Another heavy *boom* through the ground behind Seb, and when the monster lifted its leg this time, it caught Seb on the way up with what felt like its huge toe and nudged him forward.

On the edge of his balance, Seb yelled as he teetered on the brink, clumsy in his forward momentum. When his right foot caught around the heel of his left, Seb fell, hit the ground so hard it ran a violent shake through his frame, and slid toward the hole.

Seb came up a metre or two short of the tunnel, and the monster behind him roared again. It had stopped running, and the sound of its vicious call came close to Seb as it brought its face down to him. Even more terrifying in slow motion, the dark smoke that the monster breathed coated Seb's skin with a thick, tacky film. When he turned to look up into its cavernous shadowed mouth, he saw only darkness and shook as he pulled his hands over his face. Before he felt the touch of the monster, someone grabbed his hands and dragged him backwards.

The monster roared again, and when Seb opened his eyes, he saw the creature lunge forward and miss him as he slipped into the shelter of the tunnel.

When the huge monster crashed into the wall, it seemed to shake the entire planet.

Seb scrabbled back about ten metres away from the mouth of the tunnel and stared at the large and fiery orange eye that peered in after him. The roar, slightly diminished from the monster turning its head to peer through the hole, rattled in Seb's chest nonetheless and shook the ground. A cry of defeat; the monster had lost, and it knew it.

As Seb lay on the cold and hard ground, his lungs tight from the smoke inhalation, and so sweaty his clothes clung to him, he looked up behind him at Sparks and smiled. "Thank you."

The small girl shrugged and then laughed as her wide purple eyes spread even wider. "Damn, that was close."

Chapter Forty

With the smell of bonfire still stuck to him, Seb breathed in the cooler air of his surroundings. A sharp sting shot through his lungs every time he inhaled past a certain point, forcing him to take more frequent and shallower breaths.

They'd walked on a slow incline for at least half an hour, each step bringing them closer to a fresher breeze. The temperature had dropped a little, and they could hear the sound of the wind as it raced across the mouth of the tunnel, but they couldn't yet see their exit.

Seb laughed. "Who'd have thought that sound would be comforting?"

"I just hope we're near the spaceport," Sparks said. "I don't know what we'll do if we still have a way to go in that wind."

"We'll wait 'til dark," Seb replied. "I'll wait for a couple of days as long as I don't have to face the thing down there again. What was that creature anyway?"

"A balrog."

Seb stopped.

A few paces later, Sparks turned around to look at him. "You hadn't worked that out?"

At a loss for words, Seb's heart galloped. After a few seconds, his body shook and he blew out a puff of air that bulged his cheeks. "Damn. Of course it was. Wow, I'm glad I didn't realise that at the time. I would have crapped my pants and stopped running had I known. A balrog!"

"Come on," Sparks said, and walked off again.

Seb shook his head. "Damn!" He then took off after Sparks in search of the cooler, fresher air above.

***

"I never thought I'd be glad to see this place again," Seb said when they reached the mouth of the tunnel and peered out across the glassy onyx wasteland of Zenk. Although, when he looked into the distance, his slight relief vanished. He dropped his shoulders and shook his head. He looked at Sparks. She'd clearly already seen it.

"We're farther away than before," Seb said.

Before Sparks could reply, a deep growl shook the ground.

Seb poked his head from the cave's entrance and saw a huge transport vehicle approaching. "Do you think it's heading to the spaceport?"

Sparks already had her computer in her hand and scowled down at it as she tapped at the screen. "I'm not sure, but we have to guess it is."

She didn't say anything else; her face lit up as her eyes shifted from side to side. Her fingers turned into the usual blur as she tapped away at the screen.

Loose rocks bounced on the ground in response to the deep rumble of the large truck. Seb continued to look from the huge black transporter to Sparks and back to the transporter again.

As the vehicle passed them, Sparks tapped her screen one last time and looked up.

The transporter's engine cut out and it rolled to a groaning halt. Before Seb could ask any questions, Sparks tugged on his arm. "Come on, let's go."

Although the fierce wind stung and Seb could feel the cuts it instantly opened in his skin, he followed the diminutive Sparks to the back of the transporter. The door had a pass code, but within seconds, Sparks had opened it and popped the door free. She held it open for Seb, and then she climbed in after him before she closed the door behind them.

The second he entered the transporter, Seb grabbed his nose. A reek of manure and animals smothered him and he fought against his heave. Full of pens, the transporter clearly had to move livestock from one place to another.

Each animal had been stored by itself, so Seb unlatched the pen closest to the door, slipped inside, and encouraged Sparks in after him. Once she'd entered, they closed the pen behind them.

Although Seb didn't recognise the creature being transported, the huge animal looked like a member of the schtoo family. A large quadruped—easily four times the weight of Seb—the docile beings were traded for their meat. They had a shrill call that could be heard from miles around whenever batches of them went to slaughter.

The creature slowly turned around so it faced Seb and Sparks. Its eyes widened at seeing the pair and it drew a deep breath. At that moment, Seb's world slipped into slow motion and he noticed a spot on the creature's chest. He drove a swift kick to it, cutting the creature's call off before it could make it. Its front legs went first as it folded down onto the floor and landed on its chin.

After it had fallen, the large creature lay breathing on its side on the dirty floor. Seb looked at Sparks, her large purple eyes wide behind her thick glasses. "It's fine," he said. "It won't wake up."

Without another word, Sparks lifted her tiny computer, her face lit up again by the screen. Several taps later, the transporter roared to life again.

Seb couldn't help but smile as he leaned forward and patted Sparks' shoulder. "Amazing."

With her eyebrows raised, Sparks leaned against the wall of the pen. "We just need to hope they're heading to the spaceport and not away from it."

Chapter Forty-One

For most of the journey, Seb crouched down next to the unconscious schtoo and stroked it. The creature had seemed distressed until Seb placed his hand on the side of its warm face. After a few seconds, its breathing slowed down and its muscles relaxed. The least he could do was offer the thing a little comfort after what he'd done to it. Guilt twisted through him to look at the great beast, but he couldn't let it give them away. As much as he loved animals, he didn't love them anywhere near enough for a stretch in prison, especially a prison where every prisoner awaited execution.

The transporter came to a halt and shoved Seb forward in his crouch. He nearly fell over the large schtoo. He jumped to his feet and looked at Sparks. She'd already switched on her mini-computer and her fingers danced over the touch screen.

A couple of seconds later, Sparks looked toward the back of the transporter, and the back door popped open with a *thunk*. After one last stroke of the downed schtoo, Seb followed Sparks out of the pen and to the back door.

The pair slipped from the back of the large vehicle as quietly as they could and looked around. They'd been backed into what looked like a cargo bay. With no ship currently docked to it, the pair had an escape route.

Without a word, Sparks looked at Seb and pointed at the exit from the bay. Seb nodded and followed her again. Because of her stature, Sparks seemed to move easily without sound. Seb did his best to mimic her as he ran on tiptoes, but the scuff of his feet called out for any ears keen enough to hear.

The area beyond the cargo bay opened up into a huge spaceport. Busy with all sorts of beings, Sparks slowed down to a fast walk and Seb fell into stride beside her. Both of them frowned as they stared straight ahead, walking like they had a place to be.

"I'm glad we didn't have to wear a uniform in that prison. That would have made blending in a hell of a lot trickier, eh?" Sparks said from the side of her mouth.

Seb looked around at everyone as they went about loading and unloading ships, and breathed a relieved sigh. "I think we've made it, Sparks."

"Don't speak too soon. We need to get off this hideous planet first."

As they walked, Sparks removed her computer again. "What are you doing?" Seb asked.

Without looking up, she said, "Finding out which ship will get us out of here." After a couple more taps, she looked up from her screen at a large black ship on the other side of the docking bay. "That one. It's carrying fabrics to Ameldia."

"I've heard it's nice there."

"And we don't have to travel with livestock," Sparks added.

With the muddy, sweaty smell of the schtoo still up his nose, balrog smoke clinging to his skin, and the excrement from the hanging creatures in the cave coating his trousers, Seb screwed his face up and laughed. "There is that."

Were it not for the spaceport being full of grimy mechanics, livestock, and farmers, he might have stood out by a mile.

***

As they got close to the ship, Sparks looked up the walkway that ran through the centre of the spaceport and her entire frame sank. "Oh, damn."

Seb's pulse accelerated and he scanned the crowd. "What? What is it?"

For a moment, Sparks didn't reply. Instead, she stared at three beings in uniform as they headed straight for them. All three of them stared directly at Sparks, their jaws locked with determined grimaces, their eyes narrowed. At about eight feet tall, the one in the middle stood head and shoulders above the other two. The beast had yellow skin covered in welts and warts, and green eyes. It looked like a walking disease. To stare at it for too long turned Seb's stomach. A Mandulu walked on either side of it.

Sparks said, "Now they've seen me, they won't let me go."

"How do you know they want you?"

"Firstly, look at their faces. Who else do they want in here?"

"Okay, it does kind of look that way. And secondly?"

"I robbed them back on Aloo. They were docking when I blew their ship's electronics, broke into their private quarters, and stole all of their personal belongings."

Despair sagged through Seb's frame. "*Why* do you do it? Surely you know someone's going to catch up with you at some point."

"They saw me leaving with their things. It would have been the perfect job were it not for that. Look, Seb, there's nothing you can do. Any fuss and we're both getting caught. You go and slip on that ship and I'll take the rap. Whatever they try to do to me, I'll probably just end up back on *The Black Hole* anyway. I reckon I can get out of there if they lock me up again."

As Seb looked from the angry beings to Sparks and back to the angry beings again, he raised an eyebrow. "How did you get out of your cell on *The Black Hole* anyway?"

The three beasts closed down on Sparks and she shook her head. "If you don't break off now, they'll take you down with me." Even as she said it, Sparks had started to separate herself from Seb.

A look from Sparks to the creatures who wanted her and back to Sparks again, and Seb broke away from her. He slipped into the shadows beneath the ship he planned to escape on. As he walked through the darker parts of the docking area, he listened to Sparks.

"All right, it's a fair cop," she said. "I'm here, just take me, okay."

When he heard the angry buzz of a taser, Seb stopped dead. Sparks' scream echoed through the spaceport as she spasmed with the electric shock, and the three beings closed in around her.

Despite a desire to go and help her, the port seemed too busy. If he kicked off in the middle of the walkway, they'd both be on *The Black Hole* again in a flash.

Chapter Forty-Two

Seb kept to the shadows as he snuck toward the open cargo hold. With half of his attention on his escape, the other half remained with Sparks and wherever the three brutes were taking her. Although the harsh buzz of the taser had stopped, Seb could still hear her swear, shout, and scream as the creatures carried her off.

The disturbance distracted the grunts loading up the ship's cargo. Three of them in total, the huge creatures looked like they could lift most crates presented to them with their own brute strength. The sweating thugs stopped their work and all looked out into the middle of the docking bay as Sparks continued to turn the air blue. Maybe she did it to give Seb a better chance of escape.

Seb took the distraction as his opportunity to slip into the open ship and hide behind a large stack of crates. It didn't make sense to risk his life for Sparks. Were it not for her, he wouldn't have gotten into any trouble in the first place. By robbing him, she forced him into the fighting pits.

A rich smell of dye hung in the cargo hold. Sparks had been

right about the material being moved in the ship; he hoped she'd been correct about its destination too.

Only aware of just how tense he'd been now he let it go, Seb sat down in a dark corner he'd found and breathed a relieved sigh as if deflating. It wouldn't be long and he'd be away from the stinking planet. Once he landed at their destination and got off the ship, he could acquire himself a new identity and start working again—and this time he wouldn't fight anything. Sure, he could save Sparks, but she had her own path to tread. There had to be consequences for the life she chose to live, and she had to face them.

In the moment of stillness, Seb thought of his dad. How would he judge him now? After everything he'd been through over the past few days? He promised his dad he wouldn't fight again, and maybe that had been an unrealistic promise. Not only because Seb had fighting in him, but sometimes he needed to fight. Sometimes life required it of him. As much as he wanted to honour his dad's memory, the guy had been an arse. Maybe it would be less stress to ignore what the judgemental old fool demanded of him and get on with his life.

Seb leaned back against the wall, rubbed his still-stinging face, and closed his eyes.

***

Once the three grunts had loaded up the cargo bay, the huge monsters lifting crates big enough for Seb to stand up in two at a time, Seb watched the cargo door close.

Anxiety twisted in his gut when the ship rocked and vibrated as it started up. Maybe he'd made the correct choice and maybe he hadn't. Either way, he'd made it now, so he had to stick by it. The time had come for Seb to stop making decisions based on guilt or a perception of what his dead dad would think. Seb needed to use his intuition more and live with the consequences.

As the ship lifted from the ground, Seb nodded to himself. He'd made the right choice. It had been the only choice he could have made.

Back in the shadows of the docking bay, Seb watched the ship he could have escaped on pull away. A large space remained where his ticket to freedom had been. The changeover would no doubt happen quickly because most docking bays had ships waiting to land. Seb took his opportunity with no one around to head back into the huge open spaceport.

Surrounded by various beings of all shapes and sizes, Seb couldn't see where Sparks had gone. The inside area with spaceships backed up to each docking bay had many places they could take someone. Then Seb saw a docking bay with the lights out, and he smiled to himself.

After another quick glance to be sure no one watched him, Seb strode toward the darkened area. He couldn't have flown out of the spaceport without his friend; despite being a sneaky little thief with no conscience, she had waited for Seb in the cave and saved him from the balrog.

Chapter Forty-Three

Seb knew he'd chosen the right option, but when he saw just how many guards had jammed into the docking bay with the lights out, he drew a deep breath to steady his flipping stomach. Any one of them would be a walkover one on one, but all of them?

The guards hadn't seen him yet. And why would they? Even when they took Sparks away, they didn't seem interested in him. A quick headcount and he saw at least nine of them, probably more. The shadows made it hard to tell. No doubt the lights would be out for weeks.

Each of the nine guards had a weapon on their hip. Blasters of all shapes and sizes, the motley security crew no doubt loved the opportunity to use them.

Seb walked past the guards at first. A collection of large creatures from all over the galaxy, even the smallest towered over Seb. He had to do something. Even if he could catch the first two or three by surprise, that would make the others much easier to deal with.

When Seb walked back across the front of the docking bay,

closer this time, he watched the security guard at the front of the pack in his peripheral vision. Covered from head to toe in brown fur, the brute had huge brown eyes and a large mouth full of sharp teeth. It had a blaster that took two of its large hands to hold, and a second one on its hip.

When Seb got to within a metre or so of the hairy brute, he caught the smell of it. A reek like it had bathed in its own waste for the past week, it added to Seb's nauseous anxiety and he heaved. How did the thing get a job smelling like that? At least it made Seb's current lack of personal hygiene less offensive.

A couple of steps closer and Seb pulled a deep breath into his body. His world dropped into slow motion. One more glance at the monster and he saw it focus on him. It suddenly knew Seb's intentions. Before it could act, Seb sprang to life and drove a heavy blow between its wide eyes. The brown irises turned white as they rolled back in its head and the creature flopped to the ground.

Seb grabbed the two-handed blaster from its grip as it fell, and turned it on the next guard. With his abilities, he didn't need to murder anyone. Instead, Seb blasted the thing's kneecap. An explosion of blood popped from where the blaster fire hit, and it too fell to the ground.

On his way to the next guard, the creature raising its weapon as it readied it for use, Seb kicked the one he'd kneecapped in the face. With his focus on the spot just beneath its chin, he listened to the wet slap as its head snapped back. He'd done this enough times that he didn't need to check to see if he'd knocked the creature out.

Before the next guard had raised its weapon, Seb shot its gun hand with his blaster. The guard screamed as its weapon fell to the ground. It lifted the bloody stump that used to be its hand and screamed louder.

Because of the creature's size, Seb kicked its kneecap, which knocked it down, and drove the butt of his blaster into the top of the monster's head as it fell. By the time the beast had hit the ground, it had turned limp.

Chaos exploded around Seb, even in slow motion. The six other guards all had their guns ready and pointed at him, so he let off a blast at each. Each shot hit either a shin or thigh, and each shot dropped one of the creatures. With all six writhing on the floor, Seb ran through them and kicked one after the other until he'd knocked each one out.

Panting from the effort, Seb looked around the dark docking bay as everything returned to normal speed. The coast seemed clear. The door to the ship docked there hung open. They obviously couldn't close it because Sparks had blown the power. Like in the docking bay, the lights inside the ship were off too.

Despite reluctance tugging him back and his body throbbing from the beating he'd just handed out, Seb steeled himself and ran into the ship.

***

No one fired blasters inside ships as small as the one Seb had just entered. A planet hopper at best, it didn't have the reinforced walls that a larger ship like *The Black Hole* had. If a shot hit the wrong thing, the ship would explode and take everything with it. Despite this, Seb kept a hold of his blaster with both hands. He'd use it as a bludgeon, and if he got backed into a corner, going up in a ball of hot rocket fuel had to be better than being taken back to *The Black Hole*. Sparks might have been confident, but no way would he escape that thing for a second time.

The corridors, although large enough to accommodate even the biggest members of the security team, still seemed tight—especially with the lights out. With no blaster fire, and very little room to move, Seb would have to fight smart to get to Sparks.

When Seb heard the high-pitched scream of what sounded like a girl, he started down the corridor in the direction of the sound. "Sparks?" he whispered and sped up, his feet tapping against the metal floor.

Another scream led Seb to a door. Half-open from having no power to close it, Seb peered inside to see Sparks tied to a chair. The three officers that had taken her originally stood around her. One of them—a Mandulu with a particularly malicious face—waved a taser in her direction. "You think it's smart to rob some of the most notorious enforcement officers in the galaxy, do you?"

Despite the clear threat, Sparks stared at the officer and grinned her wonky grin. Several large blinks later and she said, "Yes. I do. With that notoriety, he's bound to have something worth taking, right?"

The beast roared, and just as he leaned forward with his taser, Seb shoved the door wide.

As one, the three officers turned to look at Seb. No more than a second passed before the large yellow one that looked like a walking virus came at him.

When Seb's world slipped into slow motion, he saw the

creature's lunge from a mile off and managed to sidestep it. But when he looked, he didn't see its weak spot. "Huh?"

After he'd avoided the first officer, the next one came at him—the less evil-looking Mandulu of the two. An uppercut to its chin and it fell to the floor. The next one took a whack to the chin too, which dropped it mid-run.

With the other two officers on the floor, Seb stared at what must have been the lead officer. When the yellow creature opened its wide mouth, it poked out a forked tongue and its sharp teeth flipped forward.

Seb grabbed the taser from one of the fallen Mandulus as the yellow mess came at him, stepped aside, and pressed it into the base of the creature's neck as it passed him. A spasm snapped through its thick body, but it remained on its feet. When it turned around again, it screamed louder than before.

The beast rushed Seb again and Seb's world sped up. Seb hadn't ever been in a fight longer than this and his ability seemed to be failing him. With the yellow beast upon him, Seb's world tilted as he took a heavy blow to the centre of his face. The pain damn near blinded him, and as Seb struggled to his feet, the monster kicked him in the chin.

The blow shoved Seb backwards and he crashed into a wall of fire extinguishers. A moment of clarity and he saw the brute descend on him again. His last roll of the dice, Seb jumped to his feet, ripped an extinguisher from the wall, and brought it up in time to connect with the underside of the yellow monster's chin.

The blow forced it back, and it seemed to shake the entire ship when it fell. Blood ran from Seb's nose and dripped onto the ship's floor.

With the three of them down, Seb dropped the fire extinguisher and ran to Sparks.

Big purple eyes and a wonky grin regarded him. "You came back for me? You came back?"

"All right," Seb said, "no need to get all mushy."

"But no one's ever come back for me. Well, not unless they wanted to kill me, that is."

When he'd loosened the ropes, Seb stepped aside and let them fall to the ground. "Come on, let's cut the drama and get out of here, yeah?"

Sparks maintained her wonky grin as she jumped down from her seat, and just as Seb headed out of the room, she called, "Wait."

Seb stopped and turned to her. When he followed the line of one of her long fingers, Seb saw her computer up on a high shelf. After he'd grabbed it and passed it to her, he used his sleeve to wipe the blood from his face and said, "Can we go now?"

"Thanks again, Sebastian."

"Remind me why I saved you?"

Sparks laughed.

"So can we go?"

A nod and Sparks said, "Yep, let's get the hell out of here."

Chapter Forty-Four

By the time they'd left the ship, Sparks had overtaken Seb. As she ran through the downed guards, she looked over her shoulder at him. "Wow, I'm pleased I gave that necklace back. Jeez, Seb, how did you take all of these guys out?"

Too gassed from the run to speak, his nose still leaking blood and his eyes still streaming, Seb watched his footing in the dark cargo bay and negotiated the downed guards on the ground.

A few seconds after Sparks had, Seb burst out into the large spaceport. The sudden change in light dazed him for a few seconds, but he kept up at a full sprint and remained on Sparks' tail.

As Sparks ran down the main walkway, she held her tiny computer up and typed furiously into it. A few seconds later, she pointed at one of the docked ships. "They're due to leave in thirty seconds. Come on, let's go."

Seb didn't reply, his lungs burning as he ran. With all of his focus on his breath, he kept up with Sparks as best as he could.

Although the tiny Sparks had opened up a large gap between her and Seb, she waited outside the docking bay when she arrived at it. Bouncing on the spot, she chewed on her bottom lip.

When Seb caught up to her, she darted into the bay.

Before Seb followed her in, he heard the moan of the cargo doors closing. A slow and drawn-out groan, it sounded like the yawn of a giant beast.

Seb entered the docking bay to see the ramp had been taken away. With no access for someone of her size, Sparks stood and stared up as a door closed in from each side of the space, reducing the gap all the time. With his teeth clenched, Seb found an extra burst of speed, scooped Sparks up as he ran, and dove through the tightening space, both doors scraping his shoulders as he slipped through the tight gap.

The hard floor in the cargo bay sent a violent jolt through Seb's left shoulder when he landed, but he managed to flip over and protect Sparks by rolling onto his back.

As the small Thrystian rolled off him, Seb remained on his back and gasped for breath. Until that moment, he hadn't noticed the stench; but now, as he lay there, he caught the rich stink of manure. As he sat up, he covered his mouth with his hand and stared at Sparks. "What's that smell?"

"Look," she said, "beggars can't be choosers. This was the first ship leaving, so I thought we'd do better to get on it and get away than wait around to get taken back to that damn prison."

Even as she told him that, Seb saw the wince in Sparks' demeanour. "What aren't you telling me?"

"Huh?"

Seb tilted his head to one side. "Sparks."

The small woman feigned a vacant look.

"Come on, Sparks, don't take me for a fool." Then it hit him, and it wasn't the smell. "Where's this ship going to?"

"Well, you see—"

"Sparks?"

"Aloo."

"Aloo?"

Before Seb could say anything else, the lights in the cargo hold sprang to life. Dazzled by the glare, he heard the *whoosh* of a door sliding open. As he got to his feet and raised his fists, blinking to clear his vision, a voice he recognised boomed through the large space. "Lower your guard."

When the suited form came into view—about ten feet tall, black eyes, a pointed nose, scars on his grey skin—Seb dropped his fists and sighed. "Sparks, this is—"

"I-I know who this is," the small woman stammered. "It's Moses Deloitte, the most feared gangster in the galaxy."

Chapter Forty-Five

Before Seb could react to the appearance of the rough gangster, bars shot up from the floor all around him and attached to the ceiling. When he looked at Sparks, he saw that she too had been caged.

Although Seb grabbed the bars and shook them, they didn't budge. His pulse raced and heat flushed his face as his world slipped into slow motion. Seb spun on the spot, but he couldn't find the cage's weak point.

When his world returned to normal, he looked at Moses. "I'm not going to fight for you, no matter what you do."

Moses laughed, slipped a gas mask over his large face, and stood in front of Seb and Sparks as the hiss of gas filled the cargo area.

Within a few seconds, Seb's head spun.

A few more seconds and he fell to the ground.

***

When Seb came to, he found himself back in a cell similar to the one he'd escaped from. Except this time, instead of a dozy

Mandulu, he'd been locked up with Sparks. The small woman sat perched on the edge of the bed, twiddling her long thumbs.

A headache clattered through Seb's skull and his face throbbed from the beating he'd taken when rescuing Sparks. He looked at his friend. "What's happened?"

"We're back on that stinking prison ship. They said they won't tell me anything until you're awake. So if you're feeling up to it, please go and shout through the hatch so they know you're up."

Unsteady on his feet, Seb stood up and wobbled for a second. The entire room appeared to move like the deck of a ship in a meteor shower.

As Seb walked to the door, wobbly with every step forward, he drew deep breaths to try to settle the nausea in his stomach.

Before he could pull the hatch open and call out, the locks on the other side of the door snapped free. Two lizard guards, like the ones Moses always had with him, walked into the cell, clamped handcuffs that covered Seb's entire fists and forearms over his wrists, and did the same to Sparks.

Without a word, the guards led them to a room at the end of a corridor.

The guards then opened the door and led the pair in. There was a table in the middle of the room and Moses sat behind it. With a grin as wide as his thick head, Moses looked at both Seb and Sparks. As he assessed them with his onyx glare, he said, "So, how are you?"

At a loss for words, Seb looked at Sparks, who had her lips pressed tightly together. For Sparks to hold her sass back said something about Moses that Seb had only suspected up until that point. The gangster in front of them shouldn't be messed with. Taking Sparks' lead, Seb remained silent.

Moses linked his fingers together, leaned forward, and rested his forearms on the table in front of him. With the same wide grin fixed on his predatory face, he looked from Seb to Sparks and back again. "Let me ask you both something."

Again, neither of them replied as they stood in the metal room. Like the prison cells, the room had metal walls, floor, and ceiling. The cold grey, combined with Moses' dark glare, snapped a chill through Seb.

"Have either of you heard of the Shadow Order?"

Seb remained silent, but Sparks raised a cuffed hand. "I have."

"Well?"

At first Sparks looked at Seb before she returned her attention to Moses. "It's an intergalactic team that go to whichever planet they're needed on to sort things out. They're a secret group that many people think are a fabrication, but they're not."

"And you'd know."

"Huh?" Sparks said.

"Come on, Sparks," Moses replied. "You've been hacking into our systems for long enough."

Sparks flushed red but didn't say anything.

When Moses looked at Seb, he grinned again. "As Sparks said, the Shadow Order is a team of beings who get things done. We're the people who get a phone call when a leader of a planet has been kidnapped or when one army plans all-out war on the planets surrounding it. We go in, we do what needs to be done, and we get out like we've never been there in the first place. We employ only the best of the best."

"And you want us?" Seb said. "A couple of low-level criminals turned convicts?"

"Come on, Seb, surely you don't still believe that. This prison ship isn't only a place where we collect bounties on wanted criminals. It's so much more. It's also the galaxy's toughest job interview."

"Huh?"

"You think many people escape from here? We give plenty of people the opportunity. We set up their cells and escape routes, so if they make the right choices—the kind of choices a member of the Shadow Order would make—then they can escape. You and Sparks made those choices."

"How *did* you get out, Sparks?" Seb said.

"They didn't lock my door," Sparks replied.

"And you didn't think to be suspicious of that?"

"Hindsight's a wonderful thing, Sebastian."

Before Seb could respond to her, Moses interrupted. "We've had our eye on Sparks for ages. What really brought you to my attention, Seb, was when you wouldn't fight in the pits. You could have made a killing."

"So none of this was real?"

"No."

"You don't process anyone?"

"Not unless they really deserve it. We mind-wipe most of the prisoners here, collect the bounty on them, and drop them back on their own planet. Only the best of the best make it through. Those are the people we employ. You'd be heavily compensated if you choose to work for us. A few years and you won't ever need to work again."

A shake of his head and Seb stepped back from the table. "I'm not interested."

"You prefer the wage of a cargo ship worker?"

"It's honest money."

"You don't get more honest than fixing the galaxy's problems."

Although Seb opened his mouth to speak, Moses cut him short. "Let me word this differently. You both have bounties on your heads. You could be up on multiple assault charges." He then turned to look at Sparks. "And you, my dear, will be hung out to dry for fraud. Working for us has got to be better than prison, right? I've seen your skill set. Seb, the way you hunted Sparks down in Aloo, and how you fought in the pit. And, Sparks, you're a bloody genius!"

Sparks beamed from the praise.

"Besides," Moses said when he looked back at Seb. "Your dad would be proud. This is law enforcement on a much grander scale. You'll be doing the galaxy a great service … and you'll retire rich."

After he released a deep sigh, Seb looked at Sparks, who clearly wanted in. With a shake of his head, Seb stroked his dad's necklace. Sure, he would be fighting, but fighting for the law seemed very different to fighting in the pits for money. "Okay," Seb said. "I'm in."

The chair screeched behind Moses as he got to his feet and held his hand out for Seb to shake. Seb thrust his cuffed hand forward, and Moses shook it so vigorously it ran through Seb's entire body. Moses beamed another toothy grin at him. "You've made the correct choice." He then shook the hand of Sparks. "Welcome to the team."

End of book one.

Thank you for reading The Shadow Order.

***

The First Mission (Book Two of The Shadow Order)
is available now.

Support the Author

Dear reader, as an independent author I don't have the resources of a huge publisher. If you like my work and would like to see more from me in the future, there are two things you can do to help: leaving a review, and a word-of-mouth referral.

Releasing a book takes many hours and hundreds of dollars. I love to write, and would love to continue to do so. All I ask is that you leave an Amazon review. It shows other readers that you've enjoyed the book and will encourage them to give it a try too. The review can be just one sentence, or as long as you like.

If you'd like to be notified of when the next book in this series becomes available, you can sign up to my spam-free mailing list at www.michaelrobertson.co.uk

If you've enjoyed The Shadow Order, you may also enjoy my post-apocalyptic series - The Alpha Plague (It's FREE on Amazon):

The Alpha Plague - Available Now for FREE

About The Author

Like most children born in the seventies, Michael grew up with Star Wars, Aliens, and George Romero in his life. An obsessive watcher of movies, and an avid reader from an early age, he found himself taken over with stories whenever he let his mind wander.

Those stories had to come out.

He hopes you enjoy reading his books as much as he does writing them.

Michael loves to travel when he can. He has a young family, who are his world, and when he's not reading, he enjoys walking so he can dream up more stories.

To be notified of Michael's future books, please sign up at www.michaelrobertson.co.uk

Email at: subscribers@michaelrobertson.co.uk

Follow me on facebook at –
https://www.facebook.com/MichaelRobertsonAuthor

Twitter at – @MicRobertson

Google Plus at –
https://plus.google.com/u/0/113009673177382863155/posts

OTHER AUTHORS UNDER THE SHIELD OF

SIXTH CYCLE

Nuclear war has destroyed human civilization.

Captain Jake Phillips wakes into a dangerous new world, where he finds the remaining fragments of the population living in a series of strongholds, connected across the country. Uneasy alliances have maintained their safety, but things are about to change. — Discovery **leads to danger.** — Skye Reed, a tracker from the Omega stronghold, uncovers a threat that could spell the end for their fragile society. With friends and enemies revealing truths about the past, she will need to decide who to trust. — **Sixth Cycle** is a gritty post-apocalyptic story of survival and adventure.

Darren Wearmouth ~ Carl Sinclair

DEAD ISLAND: Operation Zulu

Ten years after the world was nearly brought to its knees by a zombie Armageddon, there is a race for the antidote! On a remote Caribbean island, surrounded by a horde of hungry living dead, a team of American and Australian commandos must rescue the Antidotes' scientist. Filled with zombies, guns, Russian bad guys, shady government types, serial killers and elevator muzak. Dead Island is an action packed blood soaked horror adventure.

Allen Gamboa

INVASION OF THE DEAD SERIES

This is the first book in a series of nine, about an ordinary bunch of friends, and their plight to survive an apocalypse in Australia. — Deep beneath defense headquarters in the Australian Capital Territory, the last ranking Army chief and a brilliant scientist struggle with answers to the collapse of the world, and the aftermath of an unprecedented virus. Is it a natural mutation, or does the infection contain — more sinister roots? — One hundred and fifty miles away, five friends returning from a month-long camping trip slowly discover that death has swept through the country. What greets them in a gradual revelation is an enemy beyond compare. — Armed with dwindling ammunition, the friends must overcome their disagreements, utilize their individual skills, and face unimaginable horrors as they battle to reach their hometown...

Owen Baillie

WHISKEY TANGO FOXTROT

Alone in a foreign land. The radio goes quiet while on convoy in Afghanistan, a lost patrol alone in the desert. With his unit and his home base destroyed, Staff Sergeant Brad Thompson suddenly finds himself isolated and in command of a small group of men trying to survive in the Afghan wasteland. **Every turn leads to danger**

The local population has been afflicted with an illness that turns them into rabid animals. They pursue him and his men at every corner and stop. Struggling to hold his team together and unite survivors, he must fight and evade his way to safety.

A fast paced zombie war story like no other.

W.J. Lundy

ZOMBIE RUSH

New to the Hot Springs PD Lisa Reynolds was not all that welcomed by her coworkers especially those who were passed over for the position. It didn't matter, her thirty days probation ended on the same day of the Z-poc's arrival. Overnight the world goes from bad to worse as thousands die in the initial onslaught. National Guard and regular military unit deployed the day before to the north leaves the city in mayhem. All directions lead to death until one unlikely candidate steps forward with a plan. A plan that became an avalanche raging down the mountain culminating in the salvation or destruction of them all.

Joseph Hansen

THE GATHERING HORDE

The most ambitious terrorist plot ever undertaken is about to be put into motion, releasing an unstoppable force against humanity. Ordinary people – A group of students celebrating the end of the semester, suburban and rural families – are about to themselves in the center of something that threatens the survival of the human species. As they battle the dead – and the living – it's going to take every bit of skill, knowledge and luck for them to survive in Zed's World.

Rich Baker

THE FORGOTTEN LAND

Sergeant Steve Golburn, an Australian Special Air Service veteran, is tasked with a dangerous mission in Iraq, deep behind enemy lines. When Steve's five man SAS patrol inadvertently spark a time portal, they find themselves in 10th century Viking Denmark. A place far more dangerous and lawless than modern Iraq. Join the SAS patrol on this action adventure into the depths of not only a hostile land, far away from the support of the Allied front line, but into another world...another time.

Keith McArdle

Made in the USA
Coppell, TX
27 December 2020

47130131R10135